"Would You P
This Dress For Me?"

Since Kelly didn't look around, Wolf didn't bother to hide his grin at her request. "How did you get into this dress in the first place?" he asked, reaching for the top button.

"My mother helped. She intended to help me get out of it, too."

"I see." While they were speaking, Wolf industriously worked at the tiny nubbins, slipping the thin strip of material that formed the loop away from each button. Gradually, the dress began to open along her spine, revealing the satiny sheen of her skin. It was at that point that Wolf discovered she wasn't wearing a bra.

Now there was a piece of information he could very well have done without.

By the time he reached her lower back, Wolf had broken into a fine perspiration. Hey, he didn't need this kind of aggravation. He'd just been kidnapped by who-knows-whom and was going who-knows-where. This was not the time to be reacting to a woman, no matter who she was. The problem was, though, that his body wasn't listening to his rational explanations. Instead, his body was reacting to his undressing Kelly with a great deal of gusto and muscular animation.

The dress suddenly dropped away from her. Kelly gasped and grabbed it, holding it to her chest with both hands. She whirled around. "Thank you. I can handle the rest just fine."

Dear Reader,

Welcome to Silhouette Desire! If this is your first Desire novel, I hope it will be the first of many. If you're a regular reader, you already know that you're in for a treat.

Every Silhouette Desire book contains a romance to remember. These stories can be dramatic or humorous...topical or traditional. Each and every one is a love story that is guaranteed to sweep you into a world of passion. The heroines are women with hopes and fears just like yours. And the heroes—watch out! You won't want to read about just one. It will take all six of these strong men to keep you satisfied.

Next month, look for a special treat...six tantalizing heroes you'll want to get to know—and love—in *Men of the World*. These sinfully sexy men are from six different and romantic countries. Each book has the portrait of your hero on the cover, so you won't be able to miss this handsome lineup. Our featured authors are some of the finest: BJ James, Barbara Faith, Jennifer Greene, Lucy Gordon, Kathleen Korbel and Linda Lael Miller. *Men of the World*—don't miss them.

And don't miss September's *Man of the Month* book, *Lone Wolf* by Annette Broadrick. It sizzles!

Happy reading,

Lucia Macro
Senior Editor

ANNETTE BROADRICK
LONE WOLF

SILHOUETTE *Desire*®

Published by Silhouette Books New York

America's Publisher of Contemporary Romance

SILHOUETTE BOOKS
300 East 42nd St., New York, N.Y. 10017

LONE WOLF

ISBN: 0-373-05666-4

First Silhouette Books printing September 1991

Printed in the U.S.A.

ANNETTE BROADRICK

lives on the shores of Lake of the Ozarks in Missouri, where she spends her time doing what she loves most—reading and writing romance fiction. Since 1984, when her first book was published, Annette has been delighting her readers with her imaginative and innovative style. In addition to being nominated by *Romantic Times* as one of the Best New Authors of that year, she has also won the *Romantic Times* Reviewers' Choice Award for Best in its Series for *Heat of the Night, Mystery Lover* and *Irresistible;* the *Romantic Times* WISH Award for her hero in *Strange Enchantment;* and the *Romantic Times* Lifetime Achievement Award for Series Romance.

To Carlos, with grateful affection

One

"No! Absolutely not!"

"Aw, c'mon, Wolf. Don't be so stubborn!" Sam Bennett responded.

Wolf Conroe sat stretched out in one of his comfortable recliners in the room he used as his study. The view from the floor-to-ceiling window revealed the surrounding foothills of the Sandia Mountains and the city of Albuquerque, New Mexico, nestled in the valley nearby. Sam sprawled in a matching recliner facing the same view.

Neither man showed an interest in the panorama before them.

"I may be stubborn, but I haven't lost my sanity as yet. I have no intention of encouraging you in your plans."

Sam took another sip from the long-necked bottle of beer he held in his hand. "But you're my best friend."

"Exactly."

Sam looked at his stubborn best friend and sighed. Sometimes he found it impossible to understand Wolf's attitude toward marriage. His attitude had certainly not come from lack of opportunities. He was a man who turned women's heads wherever he went. He had that tall, lean, hungry look that seemed to captivate and hold their attention. His thick, ebony hair and equally black eyes hinted at his mother's Apache bloodline. He could have his pick of women at any time and yet he showed no interest in establishing close relationships with them.

In the years they had been friends, Sam had sometimes envied Wolf his good looks. Sam's Pueblo Indian heritage caused him to be shorter with a stocky build and a round face. He didn't have Wolf's brooding intensity, which women seemed to find a challenge.

The truth was, Wolf ignored most women, unless they signed up for his geology classes at the university. Sam knew that occasionally Wolf spent time with a woman who understood his need to be totally uncommitted and unencumbered by a relationship. But those times were rare. He was a lone wolf. There was no doubt about it.

Sam tried once more. "You know that I rarely ask anything of you, Wolf."

Wolf raised to his mouth a twin to the bottle Sam held in his hand and took a long swallow. With a hint of a smile on his face he glanced at his friend and said, "That's probably why we've been friends for so long."

"Dammit, Wolf. Be reasonable." Sam could feel his irritation mount. It was time to bring out the heavy artillery. "I hate to bring this up," he began reluctantly, "but you owe it to me, buddy."

Wolf slowly rolled his head on the padded headrest of the chair until he was staring at his irate friend. He studied Sam for a moment in silence before he asked, "How do you figure that?" with very real curiosity in his voice.

Sam sighed. "Because I once saved your life when we were in the Marine Corps."

A wicked grin appeared on Wolf's face. "You didn't want to bring that up, huh?"

"No, dammit, I didn't! I always promised myself that it was enough that I was there for you when you really needed me. I was never going to remind you that you owe your life to me." Sam scowled as he stared blindly out the window.

"I can certainly see why. Coming to my rescue in a Filipino topless bar fight wasn't exactly a heroic deed for which Medals of Honor are given."

Sam made a face. "The point I'm trying to make is that I was there for you when you needed me," he doggedly insisted.

"Granted."

"Now it's your turn."

"To save your life? That's easy. Call the whole thing off. That's the best advice a man could give his best friend."

Sam hit the table by his chair with his open hand, making a loud slapping noise on the hardwood. "No, dammit! Now it's your turn to be there for me when I need you."

Wolf looked at the bottle he held in his right hand. He could feel the logic of Sam's argument slowly encircling him, the bonds that had been forged between them over the years tightening into constricting knots of obligation and duty. He hated the feeling, but Sam was the closest thing to a brother he had. They'd been through so much together in the fifteen years they'd known each other.

He tried once more to find a way out of the yawning hole of entrapment that lay at his feet. "Why can't you get someone else?"

"Because I don't *want* anyone else, that's why! This is going to be one of the most important occasions of my life and I want *you* there when it happens."

"Hell, Bennett. My presence isn't crucial. Janice will be there. That's all you'll need to get through the ordeal."

"Janet."

"What?"

"Her name is Janet, not Janice. Surely that isn't such a difficult name to remember."

"It's not just her name, Sam. Don't you understand? I'm worried about you getting so deeply involved with someone like her. I wouldn't be your friend if I didn't try to steer you away from potential disaster."

Sam sighed and shook his head. He took a drink before he asked in a patient voice, "Since you don't know Janet, how can you tell me that what we're planning will be a disaster?''

"You told me she's from Boston, didn't you?''

"Yes.''

"Well, there you have it.'' He waved his hand and took another swallow of beer.

"What have you got against Boston? Janet's family has lived there for generations.''

"Aw, c'mon, Sam. It isn't just Boston. It's that whole area. It's another world, you should know that. Remember what happened when we were back there going to school?'' Before Sam could comment, Wolf went on. "We learned what Easterners thought about us. Those people thought we would be little more than savages. They fully expected us to show up in war paint carrying tomahawks.''

Sam chuckled at the reminder of their university days after they got out of the marines. "We did our best not to disappoint them, remember?''

Both men laughed.

"Remember the time we raided the dorm, carrying off as many hairpieces as we could find?''

"Or what about the time you asked to borrow your date's lipstick and proceeded to paint your cheeks and nose with stripes?''

"Or the time you showed up in the student union building wearing nothing but a breechclout and calf-high moccasins?''

Still chuckling, Wolf went into the kitchen and got them more beer. When he returned, he handed Sam one of the bottles. Once again his voice sounded grim. "You don't need to get involved with a White Anglo-

Saxon Protestant, Sam. The last person you need in your life is a spoiled liberal who's caught up in her fantasies of life out West.''

Sam shook his head. "Janet's nothing like that. You're letting a few bad experiences from college color your perspective."

"And I think you're allowing your hormones to color *your* thinking. How did you meet her, anyway?"

"Through the Bureau of Indian Affairs in Washington. I flew back East for a conference in September and met her then."

"And proposed four months later?"

"I was ready to propose at the end of three days when the conference was over."

"God, Sam. You really ought to have your head examined. You don't even know the woman."

"We've seen each other as often as time permits. We've talked on the phone several times a week. I flew back to meet her family last month for Christmas."

"And you're going to tell me that this fine old family from Massachusetts is overjoyed that their daughter is marrying a Native American."

"Did I say that?"

Wolf raised his brows. "Ah. Could it be possible that I'm not the only one suggesting caution in this situation? What did they say?"

"They were polite and gracious to me. I couldn't have asked for more genial hosts...." His voice trailed off.

"Until?"

"Until we told them we were engaged. Up until then I was someone she had met through her work, a friend, and they accepted me as such."

"But they aren't as keen about having you as part of the family." Wolf's comment was more statement than question.

"They'll come around."

"I see."

Sam frowned. "And what's that supposed to mean?"

"That her family probably has the same reservations I do about the idea of this merger. They're probably doing their best to talk her out of it, just as I am with you."

"I'm not worried about it. Janet and I have discussed the matter at length. We understand what a shock it is for everyone. If my parents were still alive, they would be concerned as well. There's some major cultural differences, but Janet and I know that together we can handle whatever comes."

Wolf closed his eyes. He was not winning this argument. Sam was obviously determined to go through with his plans, regardless of any argument Wolf presented.

Aloud, he muttered, "I've never even been in one of those monkey suits, Sam. I'd look ridiculous and you know it." Even he could hear resignation in his voice.

Sam heard it, too, and knew that he had won. "You'll look great. You won't have much to do, you know. If you'll give me your measurements, I'll even order your tux at the same time I order mine. They'll be waiting for us when we arrive in Boston.''

Wolf groaned his acknowledgment that he had lost the battle. "So when is this great event taking place?"

"June eighth."

Wolf jerked up, throwing the chair into an upright position. "June! Dammit, Sam, you *know* I spend the summers in the mountains. Why would you pick such a ridiculous time to get married?"

"June is a traditional month to get married."

"And when in hell did you become so all-fired traditional?"

"Listen, buddy, if I'd had my way, Janet and I would have gotten married at Christmas." Sam grinned. "She felt that was rushing it, however. She wanted a few months to plan a wedding."

"But June! You know how much I look forward to my summers."

"It will only be a couple of days out of your summer, Wolf. Give me a break here."

"I just can't believe you'd go through with something so insane," Wolf muttered, leaning back into the chair until he was almost horizontal once more.

"So you'll do it?" Sam asked, determined to get a commitment from Wolf.

"You know, Sam, a friend in need is a real pain in the—"

"Hey, man, don't take it so hard. I'll be glad to return the favor and be best man at *your* wedding!"

"That'll be the day and you know it!"

"C'mon, Wolf. You know that sooner or later you're going to bite the bullet and get married."

"Never."

"You intend to spend your life alone?"

"You got it. I like my life exactly the way it is."

"Sure you do."

"Damn right. I don't need somebody telling me what to do, how to do it, when to do it, and to point out how I could have done it better. If you insist on living that way, go ahead, but don't try to convince me you're improving your lot in life, because I won't buy it."

"And where did you get to be such an expert on marriage?" Sam asked with considerable interest.

"Through keen observation. I've yet to see a married couple where both are happy with their situation."

"I know of several. For an example, my folks had a great relationship. They were married almost thirty-five years when he died. I've always thought my mother only lasted another year because she was so miserable without him."

Wolf didn't reply. There were exceptions to every rule. He had no intention of making a list of all the people he knew who were going through the motions of a happy marriage.

They sat in silence—Sam feeling relieved to have twisted a grudging agreement out of his friend, Wolf wishing he'd never gone into that damned topless bar in the Philippines!

Janet was only minutes away from having dinner ready when her sister, Kelly, arrived at their Washington, D.C., apartment.

"Is that you?" she questioned when she heard the front door slam.

"How did you guess?" was the laconic response. "I'm the only other person who has a key to this place, you know."

Janet paused in the kitchen doorway and took in the vision of her impeccably garbed little sister.

Actually *little* was a misnomer, since Kelly was almost nine inches over five feet, while Janet had to stretch to reach five feet three inches tall. Janet had always admired Kelly's height because she could wear so many different styles. Janet had to choose her clothes carefully so that she didn't emphasize her lack of stature.

"It's really difficult for me to understand how you can put in a day at work and come away looking as though you had just gotten dressed."

Kelly reached up and pulled the pins out of her flaming red hair, allowing it to tumble around her shoulders with a sigh of relief. "Honey, I work hard at maintaining my image, believe me." She stepped out of her high-heeled shoes and wiggled her toes before padding into her bedroom.

"Dinner's almost ready," Janet said, raising her voice slightly.

"Thank God," was the muffled response. "I'm starved. I worked through my lunch hour." Moments later she appeared in a flowered caftan that swirled around her tall, lithe body. "Anything interesting in the mail?"

"A letter from Sam," was Janet's smiling response.

"Maybe I should have been more specific. Was there anything of interest *to me* in the mail?"

Janet shook her head. "Just the usual magazines and bills." She watched her sister flip through the assortment of mail lying on the bar that divided the kitchen from their small dining area. "You know something, Kelly, if you would show a little more interest in your social life, you might find yourself receiving romantic correspondence from time to time yourself."

"Thanks, but I'll pass. So what did Sammy baby have to say that you can repeat to your innocent sister?"

Janet frowned slightly. "After a great deal of argument with his best friend about the advisability of marrying some spoiled Easterner, Sam's convinced Wolf to be his best man. From all indications, that was a major accomplishment on Sam's part." Janet began to place serving dishes on the table while Kelly placed plates, glasses and silverware on two place mats arranged across from one another.

Kelly paused in her arrangements and looked at her sister in astonishment. "Wolf? Are you telling me that Sam actually has a friend called Wolf?"

"Yes. He's a professor of geology at a university in New Mexico."

"You've got to be kidding. Nobody has a name like that."

Janet turned away and picked up a pitcher of iced tea. "Maybe not where we come from, but from the paperwork I do at the bureau, I've discovered the name isn't all that uncommon."

"Then Wolf is also Indian?"

"Sam didn't say, but I wouldn't be at all surprised."

Kelly and Janet sat down and Kelly reached for one of the serving dishes. "What does Wolf have against us Easterners?"

"I'm not really certain, but I think it has something to do with some of his experiences while going to school. He thinks mixed-culture matches are headed for disaster."

Kelly placed her fork on her plate. "But he doesn't even know you!"

Janet smiled. "He's just concerned for his friend, Kelly. You have to admire his loyalty."

"He sounds like a bigot to me."

"Regardless, he's Sam's best friend and Sam wanted him at the wedding. I'm glad he finally agreed to take part in it, for Sam's sake."

Kelly was silent for several minutes before she smiled and said, "It's going to be fun watching Mom and Dad's expressions when they meet this Wolf character."

"Kelly, the folks aren't that bad. It was just a shock for them at first, discovering that I wanted to marry Sam."

"Oh, I know. It was perfectly all right to have him to dinner, just not all right to crawl into bed with him."

"Kelly!"

"You know what I mean."

"They just hadn't expected me to be so certain so soon that Sam was who I wanted."

Kelly gave a theatrical sigh. "Ah, but when the thunderbolt hit, neither of you could resist. It was Kismet, it was in the stars, it was—"

"Cut it out. I realize that you don't believe in love at first sight, and I have to admit that I've never given the matter much thought myself. But when it happens to you, you'll see what I—"

"Whoa, whoa, wait a minute. You're the one with romance on the brain, sister mine. I have no intention of getting caught up in the brain-dissolving lunacy that people call falling in love."

"I beg your pardon?" Janet said in a frosty voice.

"Oops. Present company excepted, of course. Anyone can see by just being around you and Sam that you're crazy about—oops, poor choice of words—that you are truly taken with one another. Besides, you have a great deal in common. You've always been fascinated by anything connected with our Native American culture. Why any of our family should be surprised that you've decided to marry one is—"

"Wait just a minute. I am not marrying Sam because he's Indian. I'm marrying him because I am very much in love with him and for no other reason."

"It also helps that both of you work for the same government agency."

"Well, yes, it does. I hope by June I'll be able to get a transfer to the Durango office where he's working."

"And if you can't?"

"I'll move anyway. Surely I'll be able to find something in my field in that area."

"Did you ever think about suggesting that *he* request the transfer, and not you?"

"We talked about it."

"And?"

"I was the one who wanted to move. I'd love to live out West and get a chance to see more of our country. There's so much to see within a day's drive of Durango. I can hardly wait."

Glumly, Kelly put her fork on her plate. "You know I finally admitted to myself that I'm not handling your getting married nearly as well as I thought I was. I mean, I'm really happy for you and all that and, theoretically, I've always known that someday one or both of us would decide to marry, but I suppose I always saw that happening somewhere in the far distant future." She reached over and began to turn her glass absently. "I still remember how excited I was to find work here in Washington so soon after I graduated so that I could move in with you. It was like a dream come true." She sighed. "I never thought that when you decided to marry you would end up moving so far away. Not only am I losing a roommate, but I'm also losing my one and only sister as well as my best friend, all at the same time." She shook her head. "I don't feel at all adult about this situation at the moment, you know. I have this urge to fall to the floor, to kick and scream and beg you not to leave me."

"Just like you did the year I started first grade and left you at home."

The two women smiled at each other, their eyes misty.

Janet got up and walked around the table, then hugged Kelly. "We don't have to treat this as though I'm dying. It's such a happy time for me."

Kelly nodded. "I know. It's just taking me longer to adjust to the idea than I would have guessed."

Janet straightened and absently began to clear the table. "Just think. Now you can plan to come visit me in Colorado. Who knows? You might decide you like it so well that you'll move out there."

Kelly managed a choked laugh. "Somehow I doubt that. It would be tough to work for a U.S. representative from Maryland out in the wild, wild West."

"Who knows? Maybe something or somebody will come along to change your mind. Stranger things have happened, you know."

By June Kelly considered herself reconciled to Janet's marriage. She had gotten to know Sam much better during the many visits he made to Janet all spring and knew that if it were up to Sam, her sister would have a perfect life.

Unfortunately, nothing that she had heard about Wolf had done anything to change her opinion of him. He sounded like an arrogant jerk. She certainly wasn't looking forward to meeting him.

When she first saw him, Kelly felt no need to revise her opinion of him.

It was the day before Janet and Sam's wedding. Janet had gone to the airport to meet the plane. Sam had delayed his arrival so that he would arrive at the same time as Wolf. Janet had been concerned that they were leaving their arrival so late. So many things could happen at the last minute to delay their plans.

However, Sam had explained that Wolf refused to come any sooner than was absolutely necessary. Wolf's selfish attitude had done nothing to endear him to Kelly, even though Janet had accepted Sam's explanations with a certain resignation that irritated Kelly. Was this going to be an example of how their relationship would work? Would Janet invariably accept and agree to whatever Sam wanted?

Kelly could scarcely believe the change in her formerly independent sister and could only surmise that being in love did something awful to the brain, somehow turning it to mush.

Janet had invited Kelly to accompany her to the airport but Kelly had no desire to meet the object of her anger any sooner than was absolutely necessary. It was enough that they were going to be paired off as the best man and maid of honor during the rehearsal tonight and the wedding tomorrow. So she had elected to stay home and help her mother get ready for the added company the wedding had brought.

When Janet and Sam walked into the living room with a tall, dark, dangerous-looking stranger, Kelly knew that he must be the arrogant Wolf.

She glanced at the flower arrangement she'd been working on and discovered that the baby's breath she held was shaking as though caught in a brisk breeze. She kept her eyes on the arrangement and tried to concentrate. She could handle herself with anyone.

There was no reason to be nervous about meeting this particular man.

"Kelly! I want to introduce you to Dr. Wolf Conroe. Wolf, this is my sister, Kelly Corcoran."

Kelly turned away from the flowers. She had to tilt her head to meet his black-eyed gaze. She wasn't used to looking up to men.

Wolf took her hand and said, "I'm pleased to meet you, Kelly. I would never have guessed you and Janet are sisters. I'm probably not the first person to point out that you don't look much alike. Both lovely, but so very different."

He certainly can be charming, she thought. The look of admiration in his eyes appeared sincere and the deep tones of his voice played havoc with her peace of mind.

Kelly stiffened. Hadn't she already guessed that the man must have something going for him for Sam to be so fond of him? She would just have to steel herself against him. She would have to let him know in no uncertain terms that she, for one, was not fooled for a minute by that supercilious sincerity of his.

She glanced over at Janet before meeting his gaze. "No, you're not the first, Dr. Conroe." With an impish smile she added, "When we were kids, we used to argue about which one of us was adopted." She unobtrusively withdrew her hand from his and, childlike, hid it behind her back. She found that being close to him was a little daunting.

Janet laughed before adding, "I haven't thought about that in years, sis." She leaned into Sam so that she rested against his chest. "You can imagine my chagrin when I stopped growing and Janet continued to shoot upward.''

''How about the way *I* felt? For years I'd enjoyed the advantage of having your outgrown clothes to wear as well as my new things, only to end up giving *you* my favorite dresses a few months after I got them!''

''Mother explained that my blond and blue-eyed self came from her side of the family, while Kelly looks like our father's sisters and his mother. I think there's a family secret regarding our grandmother's having been on the stage when Grandfather first saw her.''

Kelly could feel her cheeks heating. ''C'mon, Janet, don't start with those old tales.''

Janet winked at Wolf. ''Kelly supposedly looks just like Grandmother Corcoran did at the same age.''

Wolf still hadn't managed to get his breath back from the shock he received when he walked into the room and saw Kelly Corcoran for the first time.

Had he given the matter any thought, he would have assumed that Kelly looked like Janet. Janet was attractive, but her sister had taken his breath away. She looked like a Las Vegas showgirl—with her vibrantly red hair, her tall, curvaceous body and her long, elegantly shaped legs. And those eyes. A man could drown in that sea-green, enigmatic gaze.

Kelly Corcoran was the last thing he had expected to find in Boston. No wonder her grandfather had fallen for a woman who looked like her.

He cleared his throat, wondering if he would be able to speak. ''I'm, uh, very pleased to meet you, Ms. Corcoran.''

He was smooth, that was certain. A less perceptive woman would buy that slight catch and would believe in the utter sincerity of his banal remark.

"Thank you, Dr. Conroe."

"Wolf."

"I'm sure you are," she muttered under her breath.

"I'm sorry," he said with a hint of a smile. "I didn't hear what you said."

Her gaze met his defiantly, causing a slight frown to appear between his black brows. "I was remarking on the unusualness of your name," she said.

"Oh, Wolf was explaining that to me on the way from the airport," Janet interjected. "You really should have come with me, Kelly. Wolf has some fascinating stories."

"Somehow, that doesn't surprise me," she said with a sweet smile, her eyes shooting sparks of green fire.

"My mother named me Gray Wolf, but I seldom use my full name." His words were casual enough, but his expression appeared puzzled.

"Yes, well, I'm sorry I don't have more time to chat, Dr. —, uh, that is, Wolf, but Mother's expecting me to help her with a few things before the activities this evening." She started for the door, then paused. "Since we're all aware of how difficult it is for you to be a part of the wedding party, we'll do all that we can to make your stay here as painless as possible, Dr. Conroe." Kelly disappeared into the hallway.

Wolf heard Janet's slight gasp, which verified his own feeling that Kelly's parting shot had been intentional and said in an effort to wound. He glanced at

Sam, who looked as though he were struggling to hide a smile.

"I'm sorry, Wolf," Janet said, touching his arm. "Kelly's having a bit of a hard time adjusting to all the changes going on. Not only are we close as sisters and friends, but we also shared an apartment in Washington. I hope you'll forgive her for appearing a little abrupt."

He grinned. "I'll try to contain my disappointment that she seemed less than totally enamored with me."

Janet laughed. "Give her time, Wolf. Give her time. Sam has already warned me about you."

"Me?" He looked at his friend with wide-eyed shock. "I'm completely harmless."

Sam could no longer control his mirth. The two of them watched with varying degrees of patience as he roared with laughter. When he could get his breath, he said, "I would have loved to have had a camera just now to record the look on your face, Wolf. Is it possible you're losing your touch with women?"

Wolf rolled his eyes. "I knew I was going to regret giving in to you on this deal," he muttered. "You said there wouldn't be any problems. You said—"

"I know what I said," Sam replied with a grin. "Can I help it if you've finally met someone who isn't going to fall in a heap at your feet as soon as you turn on the charm?"

"Cut it out, Sam. I was just being polite to the lady. She's the one—"

"Wolf's absolutely right, Sam," Janet agreed. "Kelly's the one who's behaving like a child. The best thing I can suggest is that we ignore her behavior. She'll work through all of this eventually.''

Wolf glanced at the hall doorway and sighed. He didn't know what he had done or said to irritate the woman. He'd tried to be polite. He'd promised Sam and, by damn, he stuck by his promises.

But he certainly wasn't looking forward to spending any more time than was absolutely necessary with Kelly Corcoran. As soon as the wedding was over, he would be on the next plane headed west!

Two

―――――

Wolf stood beside his best friend at the altar of St. Michael's, doing his best to ignore the crowd of people who had appeared to watch the nuptials. At the moment he was fighting the impulse to pull at the collar of his ruffled shirt.

He still had trouble accepting the reality of the situation. Him? In a ruffled shirt? In a formal coat with tails? A bow tie and cummerbund? A satin stripe down the legs of the pants? The only glimmer of relief was knowing that Sam was every bit as uncomfortable as he was.

They stood side by side as first one, then another participant in this ridiculously detailed wedding ceremony appeared. There were bridesmaids and groomsmen and flower girls and ring bearers, all taking their time walking the interminable length of the aisle from the back of the church to the altar.

He had thought the rehearsal last night would be a waste of time until he discovered how elaborate the ceremony was going to be. At the rate they were going, the wedding would take a couple of hours.

Wolf wasn't at all certain that Sam would be able to fake his way through that much ritual before he collapsed at Wolf's feet in a puddle of quivering nerves.

He bit the inside of his cheek in order not to betray his amusement. *This is a solemn occasion,* he reminded himself. He couldn't imagine why any man would put himself through such torture in order to claim a wife.

To Sam's credit, he had agreed to whatever Janet wanted. It took a lot of courage for a man to be willing to go through all this pomp and circumstance.

Wolf turned his head slightly so that he could admire the stained-glass windows arching high above them. Although a great number of candles had been sacrificed to provide illumination in the church, the glow from the windows added a nice touch of color.

Speaking of color... Wolf's eyes were drawn to one of the young women slowly approaching the altar. God, she was gorgeous! Her foamy green gown was the exact shade of the large picture hat that framed her face and her glorious hair. She glowed, from the alabaster smoothness of her throat to the peach tint of her cheeks and the soft luster of her lips.

Wolf caught his breath at the sight of Kelly moving with stately steps toward him. His collar grew smaller and he knew he was going to start choking at any moment.

She was only a few feet away from him when the organ paused, then moved into the portentous music which announced that the bride had appeared.

Everyone rose and faced the back of the massive church. Only Wolf's eyes remained on the woman who moved slowly across from him, then turned and faced him. Their gazes locked and he idly noted that her lips compressed slightly before she deliberately turned her gaze away from him and toward the back of the church.

I've already gotten the message, lady, he thought with a frown. He would have to be totally insensitive not to have noticed the evening before that Kelly Corcoran found him less than acceptable. She had been rigidly polite during the rehearsal and the dinner afterward.

He hadn't a clue what he had done. He might have decided that she had something against his heritage if she hadn't been so friendly and accepting of Sam. No, her hostility was directed at him personally. But he would be damned if he could think of anything he had done or said that would cause her to treat him like an outcast, a pariah, a carrier of some dreaded disease.

If he was honest with himself, and Wolf believed in honesty, he would admit that he was hurt by her attitude. Let's face it, he hadn't met a woman before with the combination of Kelly's looks, intelligence and charm—with everyone but him—and he very much wanted to get to know her better.

Well, she had certainly made it clear enough that she was not interested. So what? He certainly wasn't going to go into a decline over her rejection. Hell, there'd never be a reason for him to see her again after today.

His plane was leaving around nine that night, which gave him time to make a short appearance at the reception, toast the bride and groom and get the hell out of there. His camping equipment was already loaded and waiting in his pickup truck. As soon as he got enough sleep after he arrived home, he would be headed south for the Guadalupe Mountains in West Texas, where he'd stay until it was time to return to school in the fall.

So, some good-looking woman had been less than impressed with him—that was no reason to be disconcerted.

Wolf forced his attention to the woman in white who advanced down the aisle to the man beside him. Janet looked radiant, and Wolf found himself happy for his friend. Sam was a wonderful man. He'd make a loving and compassionate husband and father. And Janet certainly seemed to love him. Maybe their marriage would work out, after all.

Wolf willed his attention to stay with the ceremony. He listened carefully as the pastor said the timeless words that would join these two people together. His gaze absently wandered to Kelly, and he was startled to see her eyes sparkling with tears.

The dress she wore enhanced the color of her eyes while the tears turned them into glittering jewels. He watched as one tear spilled over the thick fringe of lashes and traced a path across her smooth cheek.

Wolf found himself with an almost irresistible desire to brush his thumb across her cheek and smooth her tears away.

He was really losing it.

Okay, so he hadn't been part of that many wedding ceremonies before. Let's face it, this was the first wedding he'd ever attended, much less participated in. This really wasn't his kind of scene at all.

He wished to hell the lump in his throat would disappear.

And then it was over! Triumphant music arose from the organ while Sam carefully lifted Janet's veil and gently kissed her. The newly wedded couple turned and faced the congregation, then started up the aisle.

That was his cue to step forward and allow Kelly to rest her arm upon his sleeve. She did so without looking at him, which was fine with him. Wolf stared straight ahead as they followed Sam and Janet up the aisle, mentally counting the hours until he could get away.

By the time the bride and groom reached the back of the church, people were surrounding them with hugs, kisses, best wishes and happy tears. Wolf concluded that this was not his idea of fun at all.

Janet reached their side with difficulty. "Oh, Kelly. Would you and Wolf go on over to the hotel and make sure everything's ready for the reception?" She indicated a stretch limousine waiting at the bottom of the steps outside. "Dad must have planned to surprise us with the car, but mine's already parked out back. Why don't you guys enjoy the car, and we'll come along later?"

"But, Janet—" The last thing Kelly wanted to do was to spend any time alone with Wolf Conroe. Maybe she'd been a little hasty in believing that she could resist his oh-so-obvious charms. The next best thing was not to put herself in a position where she'd be tempted.

"I know. Daddy may be disappointed, but quite frankly, stretch limos really aren't my style. Go on! Enjoy!"

Kelly glanced into Wolf's black eyes. He must be one heck of a poker player, she decided with a silent groan. She had no idea what he thought about Janet's request.

Oh, well. What could happen in an eight-block car ride, after all?

Forcing a smile, Kelly said, "Is that all right with you, Wolf?"

"Whatever you want to do, Kelly," he said in that low voice of his that invariably caused shivers to race up and down her spine.

She turned and gave her sister a hug. "All right. We'll see you there. Try not to be too long!"

Kelly turned and, gathering up the full skirt of her dress, began going down the steps.

Wolf glanced at the waiting limousine with its smoked-glass windows. He could tell that the driver was already inside because the engine was on. He opened the rear door and helped Kelly enter, then slid in beside her.

As soon as the door closed, he heard the locks snap and glanced toward the front seat in surprise. His second surprise was to see that the opaque window between the front and back seats was up. The chauffeur must be used to couples who wanted privacy.

He grinned at the thought. Just how much could a couple accomplish in a few short blocks? He glanced at the woman beside him, who was reaching up to her hat.

"Here, let me," he said, removing the hat pin that she had been searching for and lifting the large-brimmed hat from her head.

"You really look beautiful, Kelly," he said quietly.

Her heart tripped over a couple of beats before regaining its regular rhythm. Why did he have to sound so blasted sincere!

"Thank you," she said, without looking at him.

"Kelly?"

Slowly she turned her head until she could see him. "Yes?"

"What have you got against me?"

She studied him for a moment in silence before she shrugged. "I've never cared for egotistical males who make a career out of charming their way through life."

He stared at her in silence for a few moments, then nodded. "What an astute young woman you are. You figured me out after having known me for something like twenty-four hours. Quite a feat!"

"I heard more than enough from Sam, believe me."

"Sam? What could he have said to give you that impression of me?"

"Oh, Sam thinks you walk on water. But it was easy enough to read between the lines."

"I see."

They sat in silence for a few minutes before Wolf decided to do what he could to smooth over the situation. "Look, you've made it obvious that you are less than charmed by me—"

"Ah," she interrupted sweetly. "You, too, are very astute."

Wolf didn't know what it was, exactly, that set him off. Was it that she tossed that line to him while staring out the window of the car in obvious boredom? Was it that she was one of the most sensuously attractive women he'd ever known?

Whatever it was, it made him forget where he was, who she was and what the consequences of his actions might be.

Wolf hauled her into his lap and, trapping her arms at her sides, bent toward her.

Clearly Kelly had not expected his sudden move. She had opened her mouth to protest when his lips covered hers in total and complete possession.

His arms felt like steel bands clamping her against his hard chest. Furious, she began to kick and squirm in an effort to get away from him. Frothy petticoats seemed to fill the seat of the car.

Kelly wasn't certain what changed, exactly. His arms loosened somewhat, although not enough to allow her to move; his lips softened and moved gently across her mouth in a sensuous exploration that seduced her into ending her struggle and relaxing against him.

His tongue roamed freely, tracing the line of her lips, stroking and coaxing until she allowed him entrance into her mouth. Kelly felt as though she were drowning in a sea of new and very pleasant sensations. She didn't understand what was happening to her. Her very own body seemed to be betraying her.

As though what was happening to her was no longer reality but a dream, she idly noticed that her hand was free. Of its own volition it seemed to move upward into his hair. She felt its rough texture as her fingers ran through it and she felt like purring.

In fact, she *was* purring. That disgusting pleasure sound was coming from *her!*

Kelly opened her eyes and forced her hand to return to his chest where she pushed against him with all her strength.

He didn't appear to notice.

She became aware of the rather compromising position she was in. Her dress and assorted petticoats were hiked up to her thighs, and she was being clutched in the arms of a damned sex fiend while he did something shiveringly erotic to her ear!

''Stop that!'' she managed to get out. Although in her mind she had screamed the command, her husky voice barely whispered the words aloud.

He ignored her quite simply by returning his attention to her mouth, effectively muffling her complaints.

Kelly felt reality slipping away once more as her body betrayed her by turning into liquefied heat. Somewhere in the back of her mind she knew that to stop struggling to get free from this madman would have earth-shaking consequences. But at the moment her mind wasn't functioning very clearly, and she couldn't focus on what those consequences might be.

Kelly first realized that the limousine had reached its destination when the door by her head was opened. She hadn't noticed that the car had stopped. She'd been too wrapped up in what Wolf was doing—in what she was allowing him to do—and she was furious.

"Let go of me!" she muttered through clenched teeth.

Wolf gave her a dazzling smile, his eyes glowing like radiant black fire. "Are you sure that's what you want?" he murmured.

If she hadn't been battling her dress and petticoats she would have belted him one for that little innuendo, but at the moment she had her hands full.

To add insult to injury, he ran his hand along her bare thigh as he said, "Need any help?"

She managed to slide off his lap and push the hem of her gown to the floor. "Not *your* kind of help." Kelly touched her hair and realized that her carefully coiffed curls had fallen around her shoulders.

Wolf shrugged. To be honest, he was more than a little shaken himself. Talk about spontaneous combustion! He'd never reacted to anyone so strongly before. She'd made him angry and so he'd decided to irritate her in return. He hadn't had a clue that a simple kiss could turn into something so cataclysmic. It was a good thing their ride had only lasted for eight blocks. Any farther and there was no telling what would have happened.

Wolf stepped out of the car and had turned to help Kelly when both his arms were jerked behind his back and a growling voice said, "Don't worry about your bride. We'll get her. Just get on the plane."

Wolf looked around. He'd been so caught up in what had been happening with Kelly that he hadn't noticed where they were going. They were not at the hotel where the reception was being held, that was certain. They were at some kind of an airstrip, and he was being marched by two massive fellows toward a small but sleek-looking jet.

What the hell—

Kelly screamed and he jerked his head around. Two more men had their hands full trying to subdue her and Wolf almost smiled. Almost, but not quite. What was going on here?

They reached the small steps that led up into the plane. One of the men stepped back while the other lifted Wolf's arm even higher on his back. "Get in there."

Wolf wasn't feeling particularly heroic at the moment. He got on the plane. A few minutes later Kelly was tossed in behind him. He caught her as she would have toppled over.

"What's going on?" she cried, her face flushed and her eyes flashing.

"I was hoping you could tell me."

Two of the men stepped inside the plane. While one disappeared into the pilot's compartment, the other closed and locked the door. He turned and motioned to them, saying, "Please take a seat." His gesture was made toward several comfortable-looking chairs in the cabin, which appeared more like a luxurious living room than the inside of a plane. "We will be taking off shortly."

"Wait a minute," Wolf said. "What's going on here? You can't just—"

The man ignored him. Instead, he walked over and sat down across from where they stood and strapped himself in.

Wolf could feel the vibration of the plane and realized that, like it or not, they were going to be airborne very shortly.

He grabbed Kelly by the arm and led her to a small two-seated sofa. Easing her down beside him, he fumbled for the straps and made sure they were both fastened in.

"What do you think you're doing?" she asked furiously, fighting his hands.

"Trying to make certain you're safe," he hissed between his teeth. "What does it look like I'm doing?"

"Kidnapping me!"

"Me! What are you talking about? I don't know any more about what's going on than you do!"

"This is ridiculous! We're supposed to be at the reception! We're supposed to—" Her eyes widened and she stared at Wolf in horror. "They must think we're Sam and Janet! They were supposed to be in the limousine. We—"

"You don't suppose this is your dad's idea of a joke, do you? Maybe he planned a surprise honeymoon for them or something?"

"Oh, surely not. Dad would never do something so off-the-wall. Besides, he would have told someone—"

"Who says he didn't tell someone? He just didn't happen to mention it to us!"

She closed her eyes for a moment before saying slowly, "Does this mean that we're going on Sam and Janet's honeymoon in their place?"

Wolf glanced around the plane once more. It held more luxuries than he'd ever seen contained in such a small area. The man across from them had his eyes closed, looking for all the world as though he were asleep. He was paying absolutely no attention to them.

Wolf studied the man and realized that, like the other three men who had grabbed them, he was Hispanic. He was dressed with style and taste, but like the others, he looked more like a bouncer than a businessman.

"Are you a friend of Lloyd Corcoran?" Wolf asked, raising his voice.

The man slowly opened one eye and frowned. "Never heard of him." He closed his eye.

Wolf didn't like the sound of this at all. If this was supposed to be some glamorous getaway honeymoon, there would be no need to use force. He rubbed his arm. They had definitely used force.

So what was going on?

He glanced out the small window near the sofa and watched as the greenery fell below and behind them.

Whatever was going on, they were airborne.

"If this is your idea of a joke, Wolf Conroe, I am not amused."

"Why do you think I have anything to do with this?"

"Because you are sneaky and underhanded, that's why."

"Oh, that's right, and you're such an excellent judge of character. I keep forgetting that."

"It doesn't take much talent to figure you out. I want you to leave me alone from now on, do you hear me? I don't want to talk to you; I don't even want to hear the sound of your voice. I just want to go home."

"Well, that's really too bad, Dorothy, because I have a strong hunch that we're both being whisked off to Oz!"

Three

———

Wolf continued to stare out the window with a feeling of disbelief. What in the hell was happening? And why?

Eventually the plane leveled off and the man across from them finally spoke, looking at Kelly. "There's a change of clothes for you in the back. We didn't figure you'd want to travel in your wedding clothes."

"Who are you?" Kelly asked. "And where are we going?"

"Who I am isn't important. And you will find out where we're going soon enough. In the meantime, may I suggest you change into something a little less formal?"

Kelly knew that for the time being she might as well go along with this character. If her father was behind all this, though, she would never forgive him. To make matters worse, if her father *had* planned this, he had planned it for Janet and her new husband, certainly not for Kelly and Wolf.

"Just wait until I get my hands on him," she muttered, unfastening her seat belt.

"Who are you talking about?"

"My father!"

"I don't think this has anything to do with him," Wolf said in a low voice. "Whatever is going on, I don't think we're on our way to a secluded honeymoon."

"I certainly hope not! Especially with you."

"Why am I having such a difficult time believing that you have such an aversion to me? I distinctly remember getting a very warm response back there in the car."

Kelly ignored him and stalked to the compartment in the back of the plane. She stared at the thin cotton dress laid out on the bed. Sandals lay on the floor beside the bed.

This was crazy. Absolutely crazy. Who in the world would expect her to wear such an awful, cheap-looking dress? Anyone who knew her would know that she would never, ever wear pink. And sandals! She *detested* sandals.

If this was somebody's idea of a joke, they had a very peculiar sense of humor.

It was only when she reached up to unfasten her dress that Kelly remembered the tiny row of buttons that ran from her neck to her hips. Her mother had helped her get into the dress, and they had laughed about the fact she would need help getting out of it, as well. She didn't know how long she stood there mentally counting in an effort to get a grip on her frustration before she finally stepped into the main compartment and said, "Wolf, would you come here for a moment, please?"

He'd been gazing out the window and glanced up in obvious surprise that she would be requesting anything from him. "Is there a problem?"

She forced herself to smile at both men impartially before saying, "Nothing major. Just an inconvenience."

Wolf leisurely unfastened his seat belt and slowly came to his feet. He was certainly taking his own sweet time about it! "What's the problem?"

She disappeared into the small sleeping area, and when she saw that he had followed her she turned her back. "Would you please unbutton this dress for me?"

Since she didn't look around, Wolf didn't bother to hide his grin. He wondered what it had taken for her to swallow enough of her pride to ask for help. "How did you get into this thing?" he asked, reaching for the top button.

"My mother helped. She intended to help me to get out of it."

"I see." All the while they were speaking, Wolf industriously worked at the tiny little nubbins, slipping the thin strip of material that formed a loop away from each one.

Gradually the dress began to open along her spine, revealing the satiny sheen of her unblemished skin. It was at that point that Wolf discovered she wasn't wearing a bra.

Now there was a piece of information he could very well have done without.

His knuckles continued to brush against the slight indentation of her spine, and he noticed a shiver race across her skin. No matter how much she pretended, it was apparent to Wolf that she wasn't totally unaffected by his helping her to undress. He found that thought somewhat reassuring, considering his present frame of mind.

"Aren't you through yet?" she finally asked into the silence that was only broken by their breathing.

"No. There must be a hundred buttons on this thing."

"I don't know. I never counted them."

By the time he reached her lower back, Wolf had broken into a fine perspiration. Hey, he didn't need this kind of aggravation. He'd just been kidnapped by who knows whom going who knows where. This was not the time to be reacting to a woman, no matter who she was. The problem was, his body wasn't listening to his rational explanations. Instead, his body was reacting to his undressing Kelly in this miniature bedroom with a great deal of gusto and muscular animation.

The dress suddenly dropped away from her. Kelly gasped and grabbed it, holding it to her chest with both hands. She whirled around. "Thank you. I can handle the rest just fine."

He looked at the thin dress on the bed. Whoever had provided the change of clothing hadn't considered undergarments. This was going to be very interesting.

Wolf sauntered back to his seat and concentrated on thinking about anything but the woman he'd just left.

Since there didn't seem to be a change of clothing for him, he decided to make himself as comfortable as possible. He took off the coat, the cummerbund and the tie, removed the studs from his shirt cuffs and rolled the sleeves to above his elbow. He couldn't help but wonder how Sam was going to explain what happened to the rented tuxedo Wolf was wearing. He had a hunch it wasn't going to get returned on time.

Wolf had dozed off by the time Kelly rejoined him. Slowly he opened his eyes and looked at her. She had found a scarf from somewhere and had tied it over her shoulders, making sure that it covered her breasts. The soft pink material made her skin glow like a pearl.

"This is ridiculous," she muttered, tugging at the knot she'd made in the scarf.

"What are you talking about?"

"Whoever this dress was planned for, she was not a tall redhead. It's at least three inches too short, and I have never worn pink in my life. It looks absolutely revolting on me."

"Honey, you couldn't look revolting if you tried."

Kelly stared at the man who looked so casual and so very relaxed beside her. He'd obviously decided to get comfortable. He'd unbuttoned the top buttons of his shirt so that his tanned chest showed in the V of the opened shirt. His forearms rested lightly across his chest. Once again, he had closed his eyes as though ready to sleep.

"Wolf?"

"Hmm?"

"We've got to do something."

"What would you suggest?"

"Overpower the pilot, radio for help. Something."

"Go ahead. I'll wait for you here."

"Me? Why don't you?"

"Because I don't know how to fly this thing."

"Well, neither do I."

"Good thinking, Red. Let's overpower the pilot and crash. There's only water beneath us. That shouldn't hurt much."

Between gritted teeth she said, "Don't call me Red. My name is Kelly, and I expect you to use my name."

"You got it. Whatever you say."

"This is like some nightmare. Do you have any idea where we're headed?"

"South."

"South? Like Florida?"

"I have a hunch it's south, as in South America."

"You can't be serious!"

"I managed to place our friendly host's accent. It's definitely Spanish."

"Oh, dear God. Why would anyone want to take us to South America?"

"I don't think they planned on taking us. This was obviously planned for Janet and Sam."

"But why?"

"I have no idea."

"It isn't a joke, is it?"

"If it is, it's a damned expensive one. I don't want to think about how much a plane like this one would cost."

"So what are we going to do?"

"Well, the way I look at it, we can sit here playing guessing games and scaring ourselves into screaming hysteria, or we can try to get as much rest as possible and wait to see what happens when we land." He closed his eyes, as though dismissing her.

"I am neither screaming nor hysterical," she said in a voice filled with irritation.

He opened his eyes in mock surprise. "I was talking about me." Once again he closed his eyes.

"How can you sleep?"

He opened his eyes. "With great difficulty as long as you insist on having this chummy little conversation." He glanced over his shoulder. "That bed back there looked downright comfortable. Why don't you go and stretch out for a while? It will do you good."

Kelly sprang to her feet and began to pace. What an infuriating, irritating, insensitive and incomprehensible man! How could he be so calm? Here they were flying away from everything that made any sense in their lives.

What must Janet be thinking by now? No doubt the rest of the wedding party had long since arrived at the hotel, only to find Kelly and Wolf gone. Her mother and dad must be frantic. No doubt Sam was equally worried about his friend.

And there was reason to be worried. If Wolf's guess was correct, they were headed for South America. Wasn't that where all the revolutions were going on?

Wasn't that where the drug cartels held complete control? Was that what this was all about? Were they being made a part of some drug-smuggling operation?

Now she felt like screaming hysterically.

So maybe Wolf was right after all. At least about this one issue. She went to the compartment in the back of the plane and stared at the bed. Actually, it looked wonderful. She hadn't slept well the night before. She knew that once they landed she would need to be alert and ready to deal with whatever happened.

After making certain that the door was closed, Kelly reluctantly untied the knot in the scarf around her shoulders and laid the scarf aside. The low-necked dress revealed more than enough of her breasts, particularly since she didn't have a bra to wear. She looked at her green dress with longing, remembering quite clearly the day the dress had been designed and she and Janet decided to have the bra built in. How could she possibly have guessed at that time that she would be kidnapped while wearing that particular dress? Reluctantly she slid the pink dress over her head, pulled back the covers and slipped beneath them, wearing nothing but her bikini briefs.

Whatever was going to happen to her later, for now she felt safe enough to sleep. She refused to admit to herself that being with Wolf somehow made her feel safer. Instead, she plumped up the pillow and placed her head on it with a sigh.

Some time later Kelly surfaced from a series of confusing images to discover that she was no longer alone in bed. She stiffened, ready to scream, when Wolf covered her mouth with his hand.

"Don't panic. It's just me." She mumbled something and he removed his hand. "What did you say?"

"What do you mean, it's just me! What are you doing in here?"

"Trying to get some sleep. The sofa was too short."

"Where's that guy?"

"Kicked back in his chair, sawing logs."

"What's he going to think, finding you in bed with me?"

"Good God, woman, who cares? I doubt that he's going to phone the news in to Danny Rather. Besides, he thinks we're married."

"What makes you say that?"

"Because he picked us up at the wedding. Don't tell me you're suffering from short-term memory loss due to the recent stress in your life."

Kelly ignored his sarcasm and pointed out the obvious. "But we weren't dressed like the bride and groom."

"Maybe he never saw them. Maybe he thinks you chose a more honest color than virginal white to be married in."

She jerked away from him and sat up. "And what do you mean by that crack?"

Wolf had been lying on his side. Now he rolled onto his back to better enjoy the view of her long and graceful back. He propped both arms behind his head. The sheet fell away to reveal his bare chest.

"And where are your clothes?" she demanded, incensed by his lack of modesty.

"Over there next to yours."

Only then did Kelly remember that she was wearing only her bikini briefs.

She groaned in embarrassment and dived under the covers.

In a low conversational voice, he said, "You're too late, you know."

"Too late for what?"

"Too late to hide from me. I've already seen you."

"When?"

"When I came in here earlier. You'd kicked off the cover and were sprawled across the bed in all your radiant splendor." Wolf was working hard to keep his voice casual. He desperately wanted to keep her upset with him. Heaven help them both if she wasn't upset. He had known he was in serious trouble as soon as he'd opened the door to check on her. In truth, he'd never seen anything that had affected him so deeply.

She'd been lying on her side, her hair spread out in gentle waves around her, and her lithe body and long legs appeared to glow in the indirect lighting. The sight of her pink-tipped breasts had made his mouth go dry. God, she was something else.

Wolf had had every intention of walking out of this woman's life as soon as the wedding ceremony was over. However, fate had decided to step in and play games with him.

Whatever was going on at the moment could have some potentially dangerous outcomes. Perhaps Kelly would be safe only if they continued to pretend to be married. Whatever was going on had something to do with the wedding. If either of the men knew that she was single...available... He broke out in a cold sweat just thinking about it.

Stripping and crawling into bed with her was a deliberate act on his part. Keeping her angry and edgy around him was also deliberate. He wasn't certain how long he could keep up his pretense of indifference to her. After all, he was only human, with no immediate plans for attaining sainthood. He only knew he had to try to maintain some control over his reactions to her.

"Were you implying that I don't deserve to be married in white?" she demanded to know when he didn't respond to her earlier question.

"Honey, you have the right to be married in anything you want to be married in. For that matter, you have the right to be married in absolutely nothing at all."

"You are despicable, did you know that?"

"Well, no, as a matter of fact, I didn't. But you have to remember that I'm not used to being around people who are such excellent judges of character as you are."

She glanced away from his amused gaze. She really felt strange, sharing a bed with him, being only a few short inches away. "How long have we been flying?" she finally asked.

"I don't know, exactly. Several hours, I would say. At one point we landed and refueled."

She jerked upright once again, this time dragging the sheet with her.

"What? And you didn't even try to make a break for it?"

"Make…a…break…for…it?" he repeated slowly, carefully enunciating each word. "You must spend a lot of your time watching television. For your information, I'm a geology professor, not Indiana Jones."

"The least you could have done was to wake me up."

"Since our friendly host out there never left his chair to unlock the door, and since neither the pilot nor the other fellow came out to chat, I assumed it would be a little difficult to escape. So why should I have awakened you?"

"I don't know. But maybe I could have thought of something we could have done. Did you see anything while we were on the ground?"

"Yes. I saw that we were being refueled."

"I mean besides that?"

"It's dark. Outside of landing lights and a small hangar, I couldn't see a thing."

"Darn."

"My sentiments exactly," he replied mildly.

"What are we going to do?"

"Get some more sleep?" he asked hopefully.

"Is that all you can think about?"

He tried not to laugh. She was so irate. Actually she was scared. Not that he blamed her. If he had his choice he preferred to have her yell at him rather than curl up into a sobbing piece of humanity.

"Now that you mention it, I can think of one or two things we could do, if you're not sleepy. After all, we're on our honeymoon, aren't we? Why don't we—"

"Forget it, you creep! You may get a lot of women that way out West, but where I come from we expect a little sensitivity, a little caring."

He turned on his side so that he was facing her. She edged away from him and stretched out as close to the bulkhead as she could get and still be on the bed.

"You'll have to forgive my rough edges, Kelly. I was never shown much sensitivity or caring when I was growing up. Somehow that got left out of my lessons in life."

Kelly heard a rough note in his voice, as though what he was saying touched some deep-seated pain within him.

She stared at him in the dim light, wondering. Did she really want to get to know him better? What if the more she learned, the more she liked him? She wasn't at all certain she could handle that.

With careful movements, Kelly turned over so her back was to Wolf.

"Good night, Wolf."

After several moments of silence, she heard him sigh and say softly, "Good night, honey."

Four

—

Something nudged his shoulder and Wolf opened his eyes and turned his head. A grinning man in jungle fatigues stood beside the small bed, taking in the scene.

Sometime during their shared sleep, Kelly had moved closer and Wolf had her tucked close to his body, his arm over her, his knees cupped behind hers.

"I'm sorry to disturb your rest, *señor*," the leering man said. "But it is time for the next stage of your journey."

Wolf could feel the woman next to him stirring. He sat up, effectively blocking the other man's view. "The next stage?" he repeated.

"*Si, señor.*"

"Where are we?"

"Colombia."

"That's what I was afraid of," he muttered before saying, "we'll be right out." He stared at the man until he nodded and left the room.

"Who was that?" Kelly asked in a sleepy voice.

"Well, let's put it this way, Snow White. I don't think he was one of your dwarfs." Without looking at her, Wolf got out of bed and grabbed the pair of dress trousers he'd had on the night before.

Being rudely awakened from an erotic dream was not his idea of a fun way to get up in the morning. Being wrapped around Kelly had no doubt stimulated such a dream. Not being able to do anything about it had his body screaming in protest.

"Where did he say we were?"

"Colombia."

"Oh, my God."

"I share your sentiments." He picked up her dress and tossed it to her. "I'll wait for you in the other room."

Kelly watched as Wolf tossed the ruffled shirt over his bare shoulder and walked out. From the time she opened her eyes until he left she had been unable to stop herself from staring at him.

His broad shoulders narrowed into a slim waist and hips, and when he stood she could see the taut buttocks outlined by the soft material of his briefs. The man was truly a joy to behold. How in the world did he stay in such excellent shape?

On some level she had known that she was snuggled close to him during the night, but she hadn't cared. She felt safe and cared for. Remembering his suggestion to hurry, she scrambled out of bed and quickly dressed.

As soon as they left the plane Wolf knew he was in trouble. Although the small airstrip where they stood was solid enough, all he could see in every direction was water. They were motioned to follow the man who had awakened them. He was striding toward a large sailboat.

"No. I won't do it," Wolf said, stopping in his tracks. Their host on board the plane was behind him. He prodded Wolf without saying anything.

"What's wrong?" Kelly asked.

"I don't like boats."

"Why not?"

"I just don't. I don't particularly care for water in large doses. I was raised in West Texas. I'm used to arid plains. Not oceans of waves."

The man in the fatigues paused and looked around. "Come. We have a long way to go."

"Not in that thing," Wolf insisted, nodding toward the boat.

The man behind him grabbed his arm. "You have no choice. Move."

Kelly whispered, "I think they're serious." She nodded toward two men who suddenly stepped out of the greenery surrounding their path, holding automatic rifles.

The word Wolf uttered was short, profane and unprintable.

He and Kelly got on board the boat. Within moments they were leaving the primitive dock and moving into open water. Kelly glanced around at Wolf, then frowned.

"Wolf?"

"What!"

"You look a little pasty."

"Somehow that doesn't surprise me."

"Are you getting sick?"

"I'd rather not discuss the matter."

"Sam said you two were in the marines together."

"We were."

"Didn't you spend some of your time at sea?"

"Yes."

"Then you should be used to being on the water."

He gritted his teeth. "I will never get used to being on the water."

Kelly hid her smile. "I see. I'm really sorry."

He kept his eyes glued to the horizon. "I suppose you enjoy the water."

She grinned. "As a matter of fact, I love it. Dad and I used to go sailing all the time when I was younger. Neither Janet nor Mom cared much for it, though." She took his hand and led him to the front of the boat. "It should be easier for you up here."

Kelly wasn't certain why she found Wolf's vulnerability so touching. Perhaps it was because he seemed so capable in the normal course of events. He hadn't shown much concern about what had happened to them the day before. She had assumed that nothing fazed him. Seeing him trying to deal with the motion of the boat made him seem more human, somehow.

She walked to the wheel to speak to the deeply tanned man at the helm. "Where are we going?" she asked with a friendly smile.

He nodded toward a foamy turbulence situated between dense jungle foliage. "River."

Ah, that explained why they hadn't unfurled the sails. She watched with interest as the helmsman negotiated the roiling waters at the mouth of the river. Only after they had successfully moved past the rough water did she return to Wolf, who was leaning weakly against the wall of the cabin.

"Are you okay?"

"No."

"That bad, huh?"

"I'm just glad I haven't eaten in a while," he managed to say.

"That's right. We haven't eaten in ages. I wonder if there's any food on this thing?"

He groaned. "Oh, please don't mention food just now."

She patted his cheek. "You'd feel better if you had something in your stomach."

"No way."

She went to the entrance to the cabin and leaned down. "Hello, down there."

The helmsman spoke up. "There's no one down there."

She glanced around in surprise. "You mean you're the only one on here with us?"

He nodded, then glanced around. "Where would you go?"

She followed his gaze and watched as they navigated the wide river that wound its oily-looking way through dense tropical jungle. "Good point," she muttered.

"What is it you want?"

"Something to eat."

"There is food if you want."

"I want." Kelly went down the steps into the pristine interior of the boat. More luxury. My, my. Someone certainly knew how to live well. She began to check the cupboards and before long was busy making breakfast.

After preparing enough for three, she quickly ate her portion and carried two plates filled with food topside. The helmsman smiled and thanked her, steering with one hand while he rested the plate beside him.

She took the other plate to Wolf.

"Go away," he said very distinctly.

"Don't be a baby." She lifted the coffee mug she had balanced on the plate. "Here, at least sip on this. You know, the river isn't bad at all. It's really rather peaceful."

Wolf reluctantly took the plate and mug from her and glared balefully at the innocent contents.

"Eat what you can. In the meantime, I'm going to see what I can find out from our friendly guide back there."

"You'd better be careful that he isn't too friendly."

She grinned. "I'm not worried. Remember, I have you to protect me." She chuckled at his groan.

Kelly wasn't certain why she was accepting all this with such equanimity. Part of the reason was that she was rested and well fed and felt ready to deal with whatever else was going to happen.

She didn't believe that they were in any physical danger. These people were obviously supposed to be delivering them somewhere, but they didn't seem to be particularly threatening.

Kelly decided to try to find out where they were going.

"What is your name?" she asked the helmsman. He glanced at her, then returned his gaze to the river.

"Jorge."

"Isn't that George in English?"

"Perhaps."

"Where are we going, Jorge?"

He motioned his head. "Upstream."

She knew that, darn it! "How far?"

He shrugged.

Obviously he wasn't the greatest conversationalist she'd ever run across. Kelly made herself relax and prayed for patience. "How long will it take us?"

"Two, maybe three days."

"Two or three days! You've got to be kidding!"

Once again he shrugged.

She spun away and went back to Wolf, who was staring at the food on his plate as though it might start crawling away at any moment. "You're not going to believe this!"

He leaned his head against the wall and closed his eyes. "Probably not, but go ahead and tell me."

"Jorge says it's going to take us two to three days to get where we're going."

Without opening his eyes, Wolf muttered, "Why doesn't that surprise me?"

"I just wish I knew what's supposed to be going on. This whole trip has been a nightmare with absolutely no meaning."

"And here I thought it was Sam's punishment of me for being so reluctant to show up at his wedding."

She pushed at the hair that fell across her forehead. "I can't remember ever having been quite so miserable."

"I can, but I prefer not to."

"It's miserably humid, and this dress scratches me along all the seams."

"Think how you'd feel if you were still wearing all those damned petticoats."

"I'd rather not, thank you very much."

"Now I suppose you expect me to jump into the river, wrestle a few crocodiles, make it to shore, capture a village of natives and force them to lead us to civilization."

"Actually, that's not a bad idea." He groaned. "No, really. I'm serious."

"Oh, I'm sure you are."

"I mean, there's only one guy. He's got to sleep sometime. We could wait until he's asleep, capture him and take command of the boat."

"And then what?"

She shrugged. "Head for open water until we're rescued." When he didn't say anything, she said, "Well, can you think of anything better?"

"Not right at the moment. It's taking all my powers of concentration to make certain that my breakfast stays down."

"I can see you're going to be a lot of help." She got up and moved away from him.

Unfortunately, Kelly's plan didn't take into account the fact that Jorge stopped at dusk and picked up another man who took over the wheel while Jorge curled up on a grass mat and cheerfully went to sleep.

By then Kelly was too exhausted to care. The combination of the heat, mosquitoes, humidity and fearful thoughts of what might be awaiting them had done their work. She fell asleep in the cabin and didn't wake up until morning.

By the end of the second day Wolf had gotten as acclimated as possible to life on less-than-steady terrain. He would never understand anyone who preferred the deck of a boat to good old terra firma. His relief when they finally docked and were told to get off was so great that he could scarcely keep from doing a quick dance of joy and thankfulness for his deliverance.

Kelly stopped beside him and looked around. "This place looks a little deserted, don't you think?"

A few grass huts stood in a ragged semicircle facing the river, but they looked abandoned. Since the boatman was patiently watching a dirt road, they turned to see what he was waiting for.

It didn't take long before they heard the sound of an engine, and in a few moments a Jeep careened around the last bend in the road. The driver hit the brakes and drew the vehicle to a shuddering stop.

The two men went into a low consultation in Spanish. Because Wolf had been raised on the Texas-Mexico border, his knowledge of the language was extensive. However, the two men spoke hurriedly and in low voices so he was unable to catch what they were saying.

Then their escort motioned for them to get into the Jeep.

"That figures," Kelly muttered.

"What?"

"Somehow I didn't expect our journey to end here."

"For which I'm devoutly thankful," Wolf responded, glancing around at the deserted village.

She shook her head in disgust and crawled into the Jeep. Since she got into the back, Wolf sat next to the driver.

"Hello," Wolf said with a nod.

The driver grunted.

"Uh, where are we going?"

There was no answer.

So what else was new?

At least he was away from the water. He brushed his hand down the front of his shirt. His ruffles were definitely bedraggled. He remembered quite distinctly thinking that he would be damned before he'd wear such an outfit. God really did have a wicked sense of humor.

He glanced around at the dense vegetation that grew wildly everywhere but on the dirt roadway. If this wasn't hell it was as close as he wanted to get to it.

Actually, it reminded him of the jungles he and Sam had trained in while they had been in the Philippines.

Maybe it wouldn't be such a bad idea for him to recall some of his jungle survival skills. Sooner or later they just might come in handy. Unless, of course, whoever was behind all this was going to meet them with a smiling explanation and send them home.

Somehow he doubted it.

Hours later Wolf noticed a glow in the surrounding blackness. As they rounded a sharp curve they came out on the side of a hill. Across the canyon was a place that looked totally incongruous in its location. The palatial mansion and surrounding wall would have looked more appropriate somewhere along the Mediterranean. Seeing it sitting in the middle of a Colombian jungle gave him the creeps.

The interior of the compound was lit by innumerable floodlights, giving the appearance of daylight.

He glanced over his shoulder. "Looks like we've reached our destination," he said to Kelly.

Kelly was staring at the scene much as Dorothy gazed upon the City of Oz for the first time.

"Is it real?" she asked, leaning toward him.

"Is any of this real? Who knows?"

It took more than an hour to negotiate the winding road around the canyon. When they reached the gate, several men appeared, all carrying automatic weapons, and spoke with the driver before waving him through. Kelly watched as the heavy gate closed behind them.

After the tedium of traveling for several days, everything seemed to be happening to them at once. The Jeep stopped in front of a flight of steps leading up to a massive double door. Wolf got out of the Jeep and turned, helping Kelly.

"What do you think?" she whispered.

"We should hear the voice of the wizard any minute now," Wolf replied.

"Can't you be serious?"

"If you insist. However, I haven't a clue about what's going on. The next time you get yourself kidnapped, how about inviting someone with more acceptable answers to your naive questions, all right?"

That shut her up for a while, for which Wolf was grateful. Although he didn't know what was going on, he certainly didn't like the looks of it. This was a very well planned operation, with many people involved. And whoever was behind it had a great deal of money at his or her disposal.

None of it made any sense whatsoever.

Once inside the towering foyer of the place, they were shown up two flights of stairs, then down two long hallways until they reached another set of double doors. These doors opened into a bedroom of magnificent proportions.

The man, one they had never seen before, who had escorted them to the room, said, "Food will be sent up shortly. You may wish to bathe and change into fresh clothing. Help yourself to whatever you want."

Wolf and Kelly stood there staring at him in astonishment. He nodded, backed out of the room and closed the doors.

They looked at each other. Kelly gave her head a sharp shake. "I'm dreaming. I know I am. Any minute I'm going to wake up and find myself at home.

This is just a pre-wedding anxiety dream. That's all. It isn't real. I know it. I—"

"Kelly, stop it! You're getting hysterical. It *is* real. I'm beginning to wonder if it isn't some sort of a honeymoon gag meant for Sam and Janet."

She glared at him. "Well, I don't know about Sam, but Janet doesn't have any friends who could afford such a gag in the first place, who could dream up such a stunt in the second place, or who would grab the *wrong couple* in the third place!"

"All right, all right. You've made your point." He walked to a door and opened it, discovering the bathroom. Without pausing, he continued into the room. "I don't know about you," he said over his shoulder, "but I'm tired of making do with partial baths. I'm going to have a hot shower." Without bothering to close the door he began to take off his clothes.

Kelly spun away from the sight of Wolf nonchalantly stripping and strode to the windows. Glancing down three stories she saw several Doberman pinschers trotting around the grounds. She shivered at the sight. Obviously whoever had planned this had no intention of letting them leave. She turned away, and her gaze fell on the bed. Oh, no! she vowed to herself. Not again. I refuse to share a bed with Wolf another time.

Next she explored the closet and various drawers therein. There was an assortment of clothes that she felt certain would fit her, thank God!

So maybe all this was some sort of hoax. She would go along with it. After all, they had been treated with courtesy. She could take a joke, of course she could. She just wished that Wolf wasn't part of it, that's all.

He was the only man she knew who had caused her to lose sleep. He was the only man she knew who could send her into a rage with little more than a raised brow or one of his sarcastic comments.

It was simply a case of mistaken identity. If she hadn't agreed to Janet's request, Janet and Sam would now be here enjoying all this splendor. Who knows? Maybe one of them would have already guessed who had provided such luxury.

Well, it was obvious that she would have to set whoever planned this odyssey straight. They would learn that there had been a stupid mistake and would no doubt send Wolf and Kelly back immediately.

At that point she would willingly agree never to see Wolf Conroe again. Never would actually be too soon, as far as Kelly was concerned.

Five

―――

"**I** have a favor to ask of you."

Kelly glanced up from her plate, having just finished one of the most delicious meals she'd ever eaten.

She was feeling very relaxed at the moment, partly because of the long, soaking bath she had taken earlier and partly because of the meal she had just eaten and the wine that accompanied it. The clothes she had found in the closet were casual but adequate to her needs. Wolf had found a pair of cotton pants that were long enough for him, a shirt and a pair of comfortable sneakers.

"What sort of favor?" she asked suspiciously, refusing to look at the bed across the room from them.

"I was told when our dinner was served that we would be introduced to our host as soon as we finished eating."

"Why didn't you tell me?"

"What does it sound like I'm doing?" he asked in a patient voice.

"No! I mean when they brought our meal?"

"Because you were in the tub at the time and had made it quite clear that under no circumstances was I to disturb you."

"Oh."

"What I'm going to suggest will go against everything you believe in, everything you treasure, everything you feel is right."

Without looking at the bed, she said, "Then the answer is no."

"You don't know what the favor is yet."

"Well, I have a darned good idea," she replied darkly. She took another sip of the wine.

"And would you mind laying off the wine? It would help if you'd stay as clearheaded as possible."

"Why?"

He looked at her in astonishment mingled with disgust. "Have you forgotten that we're prisoners here and we don't even know why?"

"More like guests, I'd say."

"Fine. We're guests, but we don't know why. And there's a really good chance that we're going to find out why very shortly."

"So?"

"That's where the favor comes in."

"What is it?"

"I want you to promise me that no matter what is said, either by our host or by me, you will not say a word."

"What?"

He nodded with resigned understanding. "I know, I know. I couldn't have asked anything more difficult for you, given your mouthy disposition."

"WHAT?"

He flinched at the increased volume and held up his hand much like a traffic cop attempting to halt the flow of cars.

"Hear me out. Since we don't have a clue about why we're here, we need to be prepared for whatever explanation is given. If you will allow me to be our spokesperson, I'll deal with whatever we're told to the best of my ability, at least until we get the chance to confer in private."

"What makes you think you'll be better able to deal with the explanation than I would?"

Wolf threw up his hands and stood, walking away from the table. "All right, then *you* respond to whatever we hear. I think we're in a hell of a lot of danger here. Since I've had a little more experience dealing with danger than you have—"

"Oh? How's that?"

"I had a few years of military training."

She thought about that. "I'll buy that."

"Thank you."

"But as far as I can see, the only danger we're in is eating ourselves into a stupor."

"Nothing would make me happier at the moment than to be proved wrong."

"But you don't think so."

"No. The security around this place is too tight. The wealth is too ostentatious. I don't know how or why, but I'm very much afraid we've gotten ourselves mixed up with some drug kingpin. It doesn't make any sense, because a drug lord would have no more reason to kidnap Sam and Janet than he would have to take us, but it's the only thing I can come up with."

"So what do you intend to do? Pretend to be them?"

"I don't intend to do much of anything. I'm hoping to hear an explanation, that's all. Even if the explanation's crazy, I want to have time to think about it. The less you and I say to them, the less they'll know about us, and I think that will be to our advantage."

Kelly could see that Wolf was quite serious. A cold feeling began to form at the pit of her stomach. She had begun to hope that everything that had happened would have a rational and benign explanation. She'd actually begun to relax, thinking that her biggest worry would be figuring out where she would sleep that night.

Now Wolf had pointed out some possibilities that she had purposely ignored. But he was right. Since they didn't know who was behind their kidnapping, the odds were that the kidnapper didn't know he had gotten the wrong couple. Would it matter to him?

"All right," she said with a slow nod.

"You agree?"

"Yes. I'll just listen, along with you. If we're asked any questions, I'll look to you to answer them."

He strode over to the table and took her hand, pulling her into his arms. "Thank you, Kelly. You don't know what a relief it is for me to hear you say that." He hugged her to him, then gave her a brisk yet thorough kiss.

They both pulled away, looking startled.

"I wish you wouldn't do that," she said irritably.

"I don't understand it."

"Why? Are you so used to women swooning in your arms that you can't imagine a woman wanting to be left alone?"

He shook his head. "It's not that. Can't you feel what happens whenever we kiss? It's like an electrical fusion, or something similar, between us."

"It's probably the static in the carpeting."

"Except the floor is marble."

"Maybe it's just atmospheric pressure or something."

"Or maybe it's our very special chemistry." He started to pull her against him once more.

"Would you stop that? I was always lousy at chemical experiments and I don't want to practice any now!"

There was a tap on the door and Kelly felt that she had just had a very narrow escape. The truth was, she knew exactly what Wolf was talking about. Her entire body started doing some very strange and inexplicable things as soon as he kissed her. She had never had reason to distrust her body in the past. Now she didn't trust her responses at all.

"Come in," Wolf said, turning to the door.

The man who had shown them to their room stood in the open doorway and said, "If you are through with your meal, will you please come with me."

Wolf glanced at Kelly, then held out his hand. She took it, grateful for the contact as they started down the stairs to find out what they were doing in the jungles of South America.

"Ah, there you are. Welcome to my home."

Wolf and Kelly took in the grandeur of the sparkling salon as well as the man who stood waiting for them to cross the broad expanse of exquisite Persian rug.

"Allow me to introduce myself. I am Corvasas Santiago." He watched their faces for a sign of recognition. When he saw none, he smiled. "But perhaps your father has never mentioned my name to you, eh?"

Kelly stiffened, but before she could respond Wolf squeezed her hand in warning. She shrugged her shoulders and glanced at the rug.

Santiago chuckled. "I must apologize for taking you away from your wedding festivities, Señorita Cantonelli...or should I now call you Señora Bartola."

Kelly's gaze flew first to the man speaking, then to the one standing beside her. What was the man talking about? She'd never heard of anyone by the name of Cantonelli, or Bartola, either.

Wolf stepped forward, still holding Kelly's hand, and said, "Would it be too much to ask why you've brought us here?"

"Not at all." Santiago waved his hand expansively. "Have a seat and I'll be most happy to explain. It must be rather difficult to be the pawns in a chess match. There's no doubt a sense of powerlessness that must be disconcerting, particularly if you have no idea why you are even on the board, eh?''

He walked over to an elaborately stocked bar. ''Would you care for something to drink?''

Wolf and Kelly shook their heads in unison.

Santiago poured himself a drink, then returned to where they sat. He sat down across from them.

''You see, Felicity, your father and I have been business partners for many years. However, over the past few months your father has shown signs that he prefers to work independently of partners, in particular—of me.'' Santiago paused long enough to offer Wolf a cigar, which Wolf declined. After taking his time about properly lighting one for himself, Santiago continued.

''I warned Luigi several times that he could not cut me out, but he repeatedly ignored me. When I heard that his only daughter was getting married on June 8 at St. Anthony's cathedral in Boston, I decided to offer the newly wedded couple the honeymoon of their dreams.'' He studied their faces and laughed. ''Quite a surprise, wouldn't you say?''

Once again they nodded in unison without looking at each other.

''I left a message on your father's answering machine letting him know that you are safe... at the moment. I am going to let him sweat a little, you see, wondering where you are and what I intend to do with you.'' He took another sip of his drink. ''Once he's had an opportunity to go over the possible consequences of disassociating himself from me, I am confident that he will be more than willing to come to some sort of mutual agreement whereby we will plan a successful future together.''

Kelly closed her eyes for a moment, praying that she wouldn't faint. Whatever she had guessed, nothing like this had ever occurred to her.

Wolf glanced at Kelly and saw that she had lost all color. He quickly freed himself from the death grip she had on his fingers and shoved her head into her lap. ''Take slow, deep breaths,'' he whispered.

She jerked away from him. ''Would you stop that!'' Color had flooded her face.

''Oh, my, don't tell me there's already trouble between the newlyweds?''

''Uh, not exactly. We've just been a little shaken at this unexpected turn of events. We'd planned to honeymoon at Niagara Falls,'' Wolf improvised. ''I must say, this is considerably different.''

Santiago nodded, looking pleased with himself. ''There's no reason for you not to enjoy your stay. I intend contacting your father tomorrow, Felicity. Perhaps he will want to fly in to make certain you are all right.''

Kelly nodded, attempting a smile.

Santiago rubbed his hands together in a gesture of enthusiasm. ''Well, I won't keep you any longer. I know that this is a time when you looked forward to your privacy. I will not deprive you of your pleasures. If you wish to have anything at all sent to your room, just pick up the phone and someone will see to your needs.''

Wolf and Kelly stood. Kelly looked at Wolf. He put his arm around her. "Thank you for explaining what's going on," he finally said after a moment.

Santiago nodded and smiled.

Once again they were guided to their room. As soon as the door closed, Kelly turned to Wolf, grabbing his arms. "What are we going to do?" she asked, her voice shaking.

Wolf stared into her very expressive eyes and knew that he couldn't kid her. "You were right all along, Kelly. We're going to have to drag out our Indiana Jones script and get the hell out of here."

"He doesn't even know that the driver went to the wrong church."

"Lucky for us that he doesn't know what Felicity Cantonelli looks like."

"What do you think would happen if we told him the truth?"

"We'd never get out of here alive."

She nodded her head. "I was afraid you'd say that."

"Let's face it. He can't afford to let us go now. But if we manage to get away, he won't know who we are or where we were found."

"Unless the driver tells him what he did?"

"If you were the driver, would you admit to the mistake?" She shook her head. "Neither would I."

"So how do we get out of here?"

He walked over to the window. "I haven't formulated a plan just yet."

"We don't have much time."

"No. Can you imagine what Luigi Cantonelli must be thinking about the message he found on his answering machine? His daughter's safely married and off somewhere on her honeymoon and he gets this crazy message."

"Well, he certainly won't be flying down to see her, that's for sure." Kelly walked over and stood beside Wolf and they both stared out the window. "I saw some dogs out there earlier."

"Figures."

"Do you think we could steal the Jeep?"

"No."

She sighed. "Me, either."

"But if we can get over that wall, I think I can get us back to the river."

She looked up at him. "Are you serious?"

"Yes."

"But how?"

"I won't pretend it will be easy, but if I can find the necessary equipment, we can survive."

"If we make it to the river, then what?"

"*When* we make it to the river, we look for a boat."

"I thought you swore never to set foot on one again."

"Yeah, well, let's get this little adventure behind us and I'll keep that promise."

She was quiet for several minutes. "You think he'll get rid of us?"

"Without a doubt."

She looked at Wolf. "I wish I'd been nicer to you when we met."

"What brought that on?"

"Guilty conscience. If I'd had an inkling that I would have to depend on you to save my life, I would definitely have been more polite to you."

"I haven't done anything yet."

"Well, at least you're making plans to get me out of here. After the way I've treated you, I wouldn't blame you if you left me here."

"Thanks for pointing that out to me. I think you're right. It would be much easier to escape on my own." He turned away and headed for the closet.

"Wolf!"

He paused, then turned, grinning. "However, my life would certainly seem boring without the aggravation of having you around."

"Thank you. I think."

He turned back to the closet. "Let's see what we've got in here. Then I'll try to get down to the kitchen and see what I can find there."

"You're going to leave me up here alone?"

"Don't worry. I won't forget you."

She watched him disappear into the closet. "Wolf?" She heard a muffled response. "Do you really think we can make it?"

He came out of the closet, pulling a dark jacket on. "We don't have a choice, Kelly. We've got to do whatever it takes."

Kelly remembered the first time she saw Wolf—was it only a few days ago? He'd looked dangerous, but she had forgotten that first impression. Now she wondered how she could possibly have overlooked that quality in him. He stood there before her, handing her articles of clothing, telling her to change clothes and to gather whatever things she felt she would need.

He had taken command. There was no hesitation in him. As frightened as she was, Kelly realized she was fortunate that Wolf was the one who was with her in this bizarre adventure.

She allowed herself a moment to thank God that Sam and Janet had not been taken. At least they were safe.

Kelly refused to kid herself. She and Wolf had practically no chance of getting out of the compound, much less out of the country. But they had to try. He was right about that. So maybe somewhere in her life she had wished for a little more adventure. Some capricious spirit must have decided to grant that wish.

Wolf pulled her to him and held her tightly for a moment. "We're going to make it, honey. Don't worry."

She looked up at him. "I'm not. I know that if anyone can get us out of here, you can."

Wolf knew better than to kiss her, but the urge to do so was almost overpowering. Now was the time for hysterics, for panic, for outrage. Instead, she was looking at him with total trust.

He was the one who wanted to panic. It was one thing to risk his neck to get out of there, quite another to endanger her, as well.

But he knew it would be the only chance they would have. Tonight Santiago was gloating over his successful coup. His guard would be down. What Wolf was counting on was that Santiago would expect them to be intimidated. After all, how many people would attempt to get in or out of this compound without invitation. With armed guards very much in evidence and vicious patrol animals running loose, most people would accept that there was no chance of getting away.

Wolf was counting on finding a way.

"Try to rest after you've gathered what you think we'll need. I'll be back for you as soon as I can."

"Take care of yourself," she whispered.

He grinned. "You can count on that. See you later." Wolf tried the door, made a thumbs up sign and slipped into the hallway, silently closing the door behind him.

Kelly spun away and began to concentrate on what they would need to survive until they reached safety.

Six

The steady dripping of rain hitting on broad leaves muffled the sounds of their footsteps as Kelly did her best to keep up with Wolf. The man wasn't human, she decided waspishly. They had been hiking for what felt like days but was probably no more than several hours.

Kelly had always thought that for a person with a sedentary job she stayed in good shape. She walked whenever she could; she climbed stairs rather than took elevators; she participated in an exercise program three times a week. None of that seemed to be helping her much in the present situation.

She quickened her pace in an effort to keep Wolf in sight. The murky green light all around them gave her the creeps. Foglike tendrils hung in the air like fingers reaching out to clutch at her.

God, she was tired! Every muscle ached, every bone seemed to creak in complaint as she forced herself to follow the tall figure hacking his way through what looked to Kelly to be an impenetrable wall of vegetation.

"How are you holding up?" she heard him say. She glanced up from watching where she stopped and saw that he had stopped and turned toward her.

She knew what he saw. She had braided her hair and wrapped it around her head. Over the hours the braid had gradually fallen so that her hair fell in long wet ropes around her face.

Wolf had found her a rainproof poncho, which protected the small bundle of supplies she'd gathered and strapped on her back. From the knees down the cotton pants she wore were soaked, not only from the rain but from the moisture that clung to everything they touched. Her sneakers squished with every step she took.

"Couldn't be better!" she replied in a hearty voice, prepared to die before she would admit she couldn't keep up with him.

He looked at her a little doubtfully, then shrugged. The casual movement of his shoulders made the heavy backpack he was wearing appear negligible in weight. He wasn't even breathing hard!

Kelly took the opportunity to wipe the moisture off her face with the long sleeve of her shirt.

"You look a little pale," he offered, searching her face.

"Oh, really? Well, you look about as green as you looked on board the boat a few days ago. I was assuming it had to do with the light in this horrible place.''

He smoothed his thumb over her cheek and rubbed gently as though removing a smudge. ''If you like, we could stop for a rest and something to eat.''

She almost groaned at the idea of such pleasure. To be able to sit down, to be able to give her feet a rest. The bliss of the thought was almost more than her benumbed brain could handle at the moment.

''It's up to you,'' she managed to say in a casual voice.

He turned, making a slow and complete circle before saying, ''I've been hoping to get through this valley as soon as possible. Once we get to the hills, maybe there will be some shelter, a cave or something, where we can rest for a few hours.''

Kelly swallowed. ''A cave?''

''Yeah, somewhere out of this interminable rain.''

''I'm not sure I want to share a cave with some animal,'' she said with a shudder.

He grinned. ''Why, Kelly, I thought I'd been a perfect gentleman during all of this.''

''Not you, you idiot!'' She glanced around at the thick vegetation. ''I hate jungles!''

''I never cared for them myself.''

''I mean, I've gone out of my way to avoid them. They give me the creeps, they give me claustrophobia, they give me—''

''Too bad Santiago didn't take us to the desert, then. Very unaccommodating of him, wouldn't you say?''

Kelly ignored him. She leaned to one side and gathered up her hair, then squeezed it until several streams of water dripped from it. When she straightened he held a large bandanna toward her.

"Here. Tie it up with this."

"Always prepared, aren't you?" she said, then realized how ungrateful she sounded. "Thanks," she muttered.

"Don't mention it." He turned away. "Let's go on a while longer, if you don't feel like stopping. Surely we'll come across some place where we can set up camp."

Why, oh, why didn't she just admit that she was exhausted, hungry, scared, lonely and convinced they would never get out of this place alive?

Why? Oh, that was an easy one to answer. Because that was exactly what he expected her to do.

She would never forget the look on his face when he returned to their room and discovered what she considered the barest necessities she wanted to take with her. She doubted she would ever forgive him for laughing.

So maybe she hadn't thought everything through. She knew how uncomfortable she'd been on that boat without shampoo, moisturizer and a few changes of clothes. Since their host had so generously provided these for her, she had seen no reason not to take them with her.

He'd sorted through the pile of things that admittedly would have taken a pack mule to carry, laid out a small brush and comb, a toothbrush and paste, some underwear, a couple of shirts and a change of pants.

He placed them in a small knapsack and slid the straps over her shoulders.

Even that small amount had grown heavy in the past few hours. She still had no idea what he was carrying in his backpack. Some food, she hoped. It was a good thing she had eaten so heartily at dinner because they certainly hadn't stopped for breakfast and she had a hunch that it was time for dinner. Her stomach was feeling hollow, but she wasn't certain whether it was because of hunger or fear.

Their escape the night before had been the most frightening experience of her life. She hadn't needed Wolf's admonishment for her to be quiet. She couldn't have made a sound if her life had depended on it.

During the hours he'd been gone he had explored the house in detail and had returned to say that it was not being guarded inside. That as long as they did nothing to arouse the sleeping servants, they would have no problem getting out.

But she had seen the dogs and knew that leaving the house was just their first problem. Wolf had already taken care of that. He'd found several juicy steaks and had lavishly fed the dogs while letting them get used to his scent. By the time the two of them had stepped out of the house and into the shadows, the dogs were sated and content to sit quietly, watching them.

He had led her toward the back of the property, away from the gate and the guards on duty there. Since the wall looked to be at least ten feet tall, she wondered how he expected to get over it.

Once again, he made his plan appear easy. First, he removed his backpack, then motioned for her to get on his shoulders. From there it was easy enough for her to scramble to the top. Then he handed her his pack and walked away.

She knew better than to ask questions. In a moment she saw him running toward the wall. She couldn't believe it. He was going to try to jump high enough to grab the top of the wall.

She shouldn't have been surprised when he made it. He hung for a moment by his hands, taking several deep breaths before he hauled himself up beside her. He barely appeared winded.

It was at that point that Kelly promised herself she was not going to be a problem on this trip. She would keep up with him, without complaining, if it killed her.

Hours later she wasn't certain which was more difficult, the pace or the fact that she wasn't saying anything about what she was thinking or feeling. When she was younger Kelly had generally blurted out every thought she had, every feeling she felt, almost as soon as it occurred. After she was grown, of course, she was selective about what she said and to whom, particularly in her work environment. There she had learned to be disciplined, a skill which was coming into constant use at this point in their travels. Who would have thought her career would have helped her in her personal life?

Not that she considered this particular episode part of her personal life. There was nothing personal about it. Wolf treated her as she imagined he would treat a military buddy, a slightly out-of-shape military buddy, at that. She noticed that he continued to check on her over his shoulder as though expecting her to fall flat on her face at any time.

At that precise moment Kelly's toe was caught under a root, and she fell to the ground. The fall knocked the breath out of her and immobilized her for a moment, long enough for Wolf to stand her up and begin to pat her. "Are you all right?" He brushed away the mulched vegetation sticking to her everywhere.

She was having trouble getting her breath.

"Easy, easy now. You just got the breath knocked out of you, that's all."

As soon as she could, Kelly backed away and wheezed, "I'm all right. I'm okay. It was nothing. I just didn't see—"

Wolf folded his arms around her and pulled her to him. "You're exhausted and I should have realized it. Why didn't you say anything back there when I asked? We've been moving for hours and you haven't said a word. I—" He paused, looking into her face. What he saw caused an ache in his chest. Tears poured down alabaster cheeks, causing her eyes to look even greener. "Oh, honey, I'm sorry. You really should have said something."

She knew that she should push away from him, she should explain that she was fine now, that she could follow anywhere he led, but it felt so good to lean against his broad, hard chest. Kelly couldn't resist. She no longer cared if he saw her tears of weakness. At the moment all she cared about was the quiet strength that seemed to enfold her and keep her knees from collapsing.

Wolf looked around until he found a spot with thinner vegetation. With one arm around Kelly, he hacked away at the leaves and stalks until he cleared a small area. He paused long enough to remove his backpack and open it. He found a thin plastic ground sheet, spread it quickly, then put up a small, round tent.

"Get in there and try to get dry, while I clear a place to start a fire."

Kelly was too tired to argue. He helped her remove her poncho, then held the front flap of the tent so that she could crawl inside. She couldn't stand up in it, but she could sit comfortably, for which she would be eternally grateful. Her feet felt numb.

It took her a few minutes to untie her shoelaces because the knots were soaked and her fingers felt clumsy, as though no longer hers to command. Once she got her shoes off, she removed her socks and wet pants. She found her other pair and pulled them on, along with dry socks. The luxury of feeling dry for the first time in hours hit her. With a sigh, she curled into a ball on her side and fell sound asleep.

More than once Wolf had cause to be thankful for his marine survival training. The years he had spent in the mountain wildernesses of West Texas had prepared him to survive in that kind of environment, but the jungle was a considerable change. That was where his military training helped, and he'd done what he could by carefully planning and packing before leaving their captor's home.

He wasn't certain how much of a search Santiago would make once he realized they were gone. What worried Wolf was how the man would react when he discovered that he'd had the wrong couple kidnapped. Did he have the manpower it would take to hunt them down?

Wolf didn't intend to take any chances. He would treat their escape as though their very lives depended on it.

After making a sizable clearing, he knelt and began to pull out of his pack what he needed to start a fire. With patience he got a small flame going, then carefully nurtured it until the blaze was hot enough that he could add some of the damp wood lying around the area.

The light had faded fast once they had made camp, and Wolf felt fortunate that the rain had stopped. At least he wouldn't have to build a shelter for the fire. He opened several packets of food, added water to a small pan and placed it over the fire. The stones surrounding the fire kept the pan upright.

Wolf hadn't heard anything from Kelly since she'd crawled into the tent. He pulled a lightweight sleeping bag out of his backpack, opened the flap to the tent and peered inside. From the flickering light of the fire he could see her curled up asleep. He crawled in beside her, then turned on the flashlight he'd packed.

Dark shadows circled her eyes. Her bright hair was a startling contrast to her porcelain skin. He hated to disturb her but she was going to have to eat something in order to keep up her strength.

"Kelly?" She didn't stir. He reached over and brushed his hand across her shoulder. "Kelly?" he repeated. "We're going to eat in a few minutes. Why don't we spread this sleeping bag out? It will be much more comfortable to lie on. I brought a blanket we can use as a cover." He waited, "Kelly?"

An insistent voice kept impinging on her consciousness and Kelly frowned. It was too early to get up. She'd just gotten to sleep. It was hours before the alarm would go off, before—

Kelly opened her eyes, startled. She was in a small, confined, dimly lit space. A large man was kneeling beside her. She pushed herself into a sitting position, wincing as her muscles vigorously protested.

"Who—? Oh! Wolf, it's you!"

"I'm sorry. I didn't mean to startle you. You were sleeping so soundly that I hated disturbing you but I have something for us to eat and—" he motioned to the sleeping bag "—I thought we could make a comfortable bed out of this."

The bandanna holding her hair away from her face had slipped off, and Kelly shoved the hair off her forehead. "Did you say something about food?" she asked, aware that her stomach was busily complaining.

He smiled. "Your dinner awaits," he said, holding the flap open. "Even better, the rain has stopped."

So at least she could be thankful for small blessings. Kelly clambered out of the tent and saw the cheerful blaze of the fire before her. It was the most mood-lightening thing that had occurred all day. "How in the world did you get a fire going in all of this?" she said, waving her arm at the dripping vegetation.

"Compliments of expert training by the United States military service, ma'am," he drawled.

He dished out a hearty stew into two metal cups and handed one to her. "Watch it. That's hot."

"How long were you in the military?"

"Almost six years."

"Were you involved in any of the fighting?"

"No. By the time I went into the marines, the fighting in Southeast Asia had stopped. But I spent most of my time in the Philippines, Korea and assorted outposts."

"Is that where you learned how to take care of yourself?"

He shook his head, his face darkening. "I grew up knowing how to take care of myself," he said, taking a bite of the stew.

Kelly tentatively tasted it to find that it was delicious. There was no more conversation for several minutes.

After they finished all the food in the small saucepan Wolf rinsed it out and placed more water in it. This time when the water came to a boil, he threw ground coffee in. She didn't say anything and he finally said, "Thought we could use some after-dinner coffee."

Kelly continued to stare into the flames without comment.

Well, what did he expect, after all. This was probably the first time this woman had sat around a campfire eating stew and drinking boiled coffee. This was certainly not her usual way of spending an evening. He knew that without asking.

He, on the other hand, had spent countless evenings exactly like this, high in the wilderness of the Guadalupe Mountains. If everything had worked out as planned, he would be there now, alone, watching the sparks of the fire spiral upward into the clear West Texas sky.

"What are you thinking?" he finally asked.

"I'm not really certain. My thoughts seem to be flying in all directions. I keep wondering how my parents are taking my disappearance. How soon everyone realized we were gone. I wonder if Janet and Sam went on their honeymoon or whether they're sitting by a phone somewhere waiting for news." She looked at him. "I was thinking how strange it is that I should end up in a situation like this with you."

"That's right. You don't like me very much."

She shook her head. "That seems so long ago. I remember how upset I was when you objected to Sam's marrying Janet. I felt you were being unfair in your judgments. You didn't even know her. I resented your attitude toward the plans for the wedding and related festivities. I thought you were being insensitive and selfish, not being willing to come when you were invited."

"I was."

"But I never thought to ask about your reasons. I just assumed you were being difficult, that you were making it clear that you considered the wedding and all the festivities trivial and unimportant."

"I always said you were an astute judge of character." He filled their metal cups with steaming coffee and held one out to her. "Sorry I can't offer cream or sugar."

She frowned. "You think I'm very spoiled, don't you?"

"Does it matter?"

She thought about his question for several moments before confessing, "Yes. I realized today that what you think of me really does matter to me."

"I think you've been very brave. Very few women could have kept up the grueling pace I set today. You never once complained."

"You laughed at me last night."

His lips twitched. He couldn't help it. "I know. It was very insensitive of me and I apologize."

"You don't have to apologize. I realize it was stupid of me to pack shampoo, deodorant and moisturizer, not to mention the amount of clothing."

He reached over and took her hand, smoothing her long fingers across his palm. Her formerly immaculately manicured nails were chipped and broken, no longer the pale coral they were at the wedding. He smoothed his forefinger along the length of each finger. "If you aren't used to thinking in terms of survival, honey, you'd have no reason to question taking whatever you expected to need." He raised his gaze until he was staring into her shadowed eyes. "The thing is, we don't have any idea where we're going, how long it's going to take us and if we're going to find help when we get there. At the moment we're on our own, which means that we've got to do the best we can with what we can carry. Those packs get heavier with every mile."

"You haven't acted as though you were bothered."

"That's because I'm used to it. I've backpacked since I was a kid. This is a way of life for me," he said, looking around. "Oh, I don't mean the jungle, I'm afraid. I definitely share your aversion to it. I'm talking about living off the land, knowing that I can face the elements and survive. When I'm not teaching I spend most of my time alone in the wilderness."

She stared at him as though trying to read his thoughts. "It sounds like a very lonely life."

"For some, maybe. I enjoy the solitude."

"I guess I'm very lucky to have been kidnapped with you, then."

"How's that?"

"I was just thinking of the men I know. They know all the best restaurants, where to buy their clothes, how to show a woman a good time. But they wouldn't have had a clue about how to get us out of that stronghold back there, and we would have been lost minutes after coming into all of this." She glanced at the trees and heavy foliage surrounding them. "It no longer matters to me that you didn't want Sam to marry my sister. I don't really care. What matters is that you got us out of a very dangerous situation."

"We're still not out of it."

"You have to admit that we're safer now than we were back there."

"The dangers are different, that's all."

"You won't admit that you saved me, will you?"

Wolf got up and started putting out the fire. "Don't try to make me out as some kind of hero, Kelly. Noth-

ing could be further from the truth. I'm just trying to
save my own neck. I saw no reason to leave you there.''

She watched him pack everything away and put out
the fire before she asked, ''What are your plans for
tomorrow?''

''I managed to study a map Santiago had on his
wall. Rather than return to the river, I decided to head
south to Bogotá, which means we'll have to cross some
mountains.''

''Why Bogotá?''

''Because the U.S. Embassy is there. I think that's
going to be our safest avenue of escape. We're here
without passports, so at the moment we're illegal. I'd
rather not get involved with the local authorities if we
can avoid it.''

''How long will it take us?''

He kept his head turned away. ''It's hard to guess.''

''Try.''

''It may take weeks.''

''Weeks! You can't be serious!''

''I had hoped to find the foothills of the mountain
range today, or at least find a clearing where we might
get a glimpse of them.''

''Are we even going in the right direction?''

''I've been following the most direct southerly route
I could.''

She looked at him skeptically. ''By watching the
sun, I suppose,'' knowing full well that it had been
raining since soon after they left the compound.

''No, by watching the compass,'' he replied in a
noncommittal tone.

"Did you just happen to have that on you at the wedding?"

"No. I searched the house until I found what I knew we'd need."

She dropped her head on her bent knees and sighed. No wonder he had laughed at her. While she'd been gathering shampoo and assorted cosmetics, he'd found food, bedrolls, cooking utensils, backpacks, compasses, flashlights. She'd been a real idiot and she didn't like the tag at all.

"Let's try to get some sleep."

Kelly looked up and found him holding the tent flap open. She nodded. "All right."

He crawled in after her, zipped the flap and flicked on the flashlight. Together they spread the sleeping bag open, then smoothed the blanket over it.

"Kelly?"

"Hmm."

"I want you to know that you don't have to worry about anything where I'm concerned."

She looked up from untying her shoes. "What are you talking about?"

"I know I've taken advantage of the situation a couple of times by grabbing and kissing you. Things have changed considerably, and I don't intend to lose control like that again. I just want you to know that you're safe with me." He gave her a half grin and added, "At least as safe as you want to be."

Seven

Kelly lay awake staring at the curved roof of the small tent, wishing she could sleep. She felt almost too tired to sleep. Her body ached in places she'd never been aware of before.

Worse, she had never attempted to go to sleep next to a man before. She had already been asleep when Wolf had crawled into bed with her on the plane. And during the boat trip up the river he had insisted on sleeping on top, out in the open, where he could see.

After turning out the flashlight he had suggested that they both get as comfortable as possible. Then he sat down on the sleeping bag and began to undress. From the sounds he made she realized that he had taken off not only his shoes, but his pants and shirt as well. They must have been uncomfortably damp, and she didn't blame him for not wanting to sleep in them.

By the time she had pulled her shoes off and unobtrusively slid out of her pants he was lying on his side facing away from her, making the slow, deep-breathing sounds of sleep.

She found a soft T-shirt in her bag, one he had allowed her to bring and, after stripping out of her shirt and bra, slipped the comforting material over her head. It was a large man's shirt, which made it ideal for her to sleep in. She had assumed that as soon as she got horizontal she'd be asleep, but unfortunately that hadn't been the case.

Instead, she tried to recall what Sam had told her and Janet about Wolf. They were good friends who had met years ago in the service, had decided to attend university together and had stayed in touch over the years since then. Wolf had done graduate work in meteorology and geology. He had always been interested in the environment, Sam had told them. When Janet asked about Wolf's personal life Sam had explained that he rarely let anyone get close to him. That information had irritated Kelly. Why would he choose to be an outcast, a lone wolf? What did he have against people?

Now, more than ever, Kelly wanted to know what made Wolf the man he was. She had a strong hunch that she would never find out anything that he wasn't willing to share with her.

Now, through no fault of their own, she and Wolf were going to be spending weeks together. She could maintain her distance from him, treat him like a stranger and count the days until they reached civilization.

Or—and this was the thought that kept her awake—she could work to get to know him—carefully, without alarming him. She could treat him as she would an animal who had always lived in the wild, free from all bondage, and perhaps coax him to draw closer. She could set about taming the wolf, at least a little. What harm would it do? Instead of judging him by her standards, perhaps she could get to know his standards, understand who he was and why, understand his feelings about life, about the world.

She couldn't rush the process, this much she knew. But what else did she have to do with her time? If they followed his plan, they would be hiking more than a hundred miles, through jungles and mountainous terrain. He'd warned her that they might not make it.

It was possible that she would die in the next few weeks, that she would never see her home, her family or her friends again. Until now, she had taken for granted that he would save them and deliver them to a safe place. Never for one minute had she doubted that she would see her family again. She'd already rehearsed telling the story of their adventure as amusingly as possible. She had refused to face the seriousness of their situation. But Wolf hadn't. He hadn't flinched from the dangers they would be facing.

All right. So he didn't want her to see him as a hero, and maybe he was right. He was gruff, and more than a little curt. He could be downright rude at times. She certainly couldn't brag about his sunny disposition. She was certain that he didn't dress with the style of the other men she knew, dance with the grace that—

Dance. They had been headed to the reception where they would have danced together. Kelly slowly closed her eyes. Would she ever dance with Wolf? She sighed, visualizing herself in her beautiful green gown once more. Wolf was there in the stunning suit that had emphasized his dark good looks. He was smiling at her and holding out his hand. Never had she seen him look so relaxed. His smile made her tingle all over.

She nodded, then lifted her hand to his shoulder. They began to waltz around the room and it was wonderful. He danced like a dream, light, graceful . . .

Kelly snuggled beneath the light blanket and drifted into sleep.

When Wolf opened his eyes, he knew immediately where he was. Sometime during the night Kelly had moved, turning into his arms until her head rested on his shoulder. His left arm must have gone to sleep, for it felt numb. Unfortunately, his arm was the only part of his anatomy that felt numb! Kelly's thigh was nestled between his thighs, her knee resting in his groin. Her arm lay draped across his chest.

After reassuring her just a few hours before that she was safe with him, Wolf woke up to discover that his words of assurance felt downright hollow. What the hell was he supposed to do now? He'd never been in such a predicament. In the first place, he wasn't used to waking up with a woman in his arms. In the second place, the few times when this had happened, he sure hadn't worried about his next moves. Since his body was aroused by her nearness, under ordinary circumstances he would have let nature take its course.

These were far from ordinary circumstances, however.

Sliding his hand down his own body he managed to hook his fingers under her knee and gently edge it away from him. After successfully managing that maneuver, Wolf allowed himself the luxury of a lung-filling breath of air. Then he eased his arm out from under her. The sudden prickles that shot through that member of his body verified his initial assessment. He sat up, trying to muffle a groan. He found some dry clothes to put on and with economical movements got dressed and eased out of the tent.

From the glimmering of light that was filtering down from above, Wolf thought the rain might leave them alone for a few hours. He gathered the charred remains of the fire together and quickly had another one going. By the time he was sipping on a cup of hot coffee, he had a better grip on his reactions.

He no longer had a valid reason for keeping Kelly angry with him, but he wasn't certain what he was going to do to keep a mental and emotional distance between them. However, some sort of barrier was a must, under the circumstances. Of course he would like to make love to her, what red-blooded man wouldn't? Even so, the idea was out of the question. Even if she hadn't been Sam's new sister-in-law, she was the very type of person he had always steered clear of. She wouldn't understand the rules of the game. She'd end up getting hurt.

Of course there was no guarantee that they would ever get out of this country alive. So what if this was all the time either one of them had? What point would he be proving by not taking what was there? Take this morning, for example. Had he chosen to stay in bed with her, he could easily have seduced her into making love before she was fully awake.

By the time Kelly came out of the tent, Wolf had worked himself into a foul mood, taking first one side, then the other of the moral argument.

Kelly had awakened in a positive mood, remembering her thoughts of the night before. She would no longer be antagonistic toward Wolf. Instead, she would be helpful and friendly and try to get close to him. She would let him know that she liked him and that she truly wanted to get to know him better.

Her first attempt at friendliness didn't produce very gratifying results. "Good morning, Wolf! It looks as though it's going to be a beautiful day."

"Hmph."

Okay. So maybe he wasn't at his best in the morning. Who said her task would be easy?

"I'd love to have a bath or shower or something. Do you have any ideas about getting clean?"

He'd been staring into the depths of his tin cup as though all the answers to the mysteries of the universe were contained within. When he'd heard her cheerful voice, he had almost cringed. But when she began to ask about a bath or shower—!

He stood up and glared at her. "You might try the Hilton. It's down the path there." He poured coffee into her cup and finished off the pot by emptying the remains into his cup.

She laughed. Instead of getting angry at his sarcasm, or hurt, she was amused! "Wouldn't that be great? I can see it now—two intrepid jungle explorers, slashing their way through the smothering thickness of the heavy undergrowth, when up ahead there appears to be a clearing. Using the very last dregs of their stamina, they put forth another mighty effort until they cut through the final thicket and discover— the giant parking lot of a multistory Hilton Hotel, complete with fancy cars, heavy traffic and all.''

She sank down beside him, still giggling, while she took the cup he had filled for her and lifted it to her lips. She gave a sigh of satisfaction and said, ''Hmm, that tastes wonderful. I may never drink anything but boiled coffee again.'' She glanced around. ''So what do you think? Is there a chance we could find a stream somewhere? I'd really like to get clean.''

Wolf handed her half of a small loaf of bread, a piece of cheese and a slice of meat. ''I haven't come across anything resembling a stream, but I'll be most happy to point it out should we stumble across one.''

She took the food and bit into it, chewing thoughtfully. ''I can't remember when anything tasted so good to me. I had no idea you had all this food tucked away. Why didn't we have this last night?''

''Because I thought we both deserved something hot to eat.''

''That was thoughtful of you.''

Wolf rolled his eyes at her determined cheerfulness. He began to break camp, rolling up the sleeping bag, folding up the tent. ''I'm not thoughtful. Just practical.''

''Of course,'' she agreed amiably. ''I'm glad one of us has the sense to be practical.''

It was obvious to Wolf that she had taken time to work the tangles out of her hair. Once again it was braided. This time she left the thick single braid dangling down her back.

"We're going to have to do something about that," he muttered to her back.

She turned around and looked at him, puzzled. "What are you talking about?"

"Your hair."

"What about my hair?"

"It's too bright."

She grinned. "I must admit that I'm easily singled out in a crowd."

"And instantly recognizable. If Santiago sends anyone looking for us, they'll be able to spot you immediately."

She shrugged. "I'll just keep the bandanna around my head. Besides, we haven't seen anybody so far."

"No, but when we get into the mountains, we'll have to seek out some villages for fresh supplies." He hoisted the pack to his back and she stood, ready to follow him. "It's not just the hair. It's all of you."

She glanced down at the plain cotton shirt and pants and the bedraggled sneakers. "I certainly don't look like a member of any wedding party I've ever seen."

"No. It's your skin. You're too pale."

"I can't help it. I don't tan. I just get red and peel."

He shook his head. "We'll have to do something."

"Maybe we can find a big straw hat somewhere."

After consulting the compass he turned away and began to hack a path through the thick growth around them. "Maybe," he muttered.

After an hour Kelly realized that the exercise had eased the ache in her muscles and that she wasn't having as difficult a time keeping up with Wolf as she had the day before. Either that, or he was purposely taking his time.

She glanced down the path at him and smiled. No, if he was moving any faster, he'd be running. Now that she thought about it, there was a definite downward slant to the terrain. She stepped up her pace, and by the time she caught up with Wolf, she heard the water.

When they came out of the jungle they found themselves on the edge of a gorge. A waterfall sparkled and fell from about thirty feet above their head, forming a pool that eventually became a stream that tumbled and bounced out of sight around the curve in the streambed.

"Oh, Wolf! Isn't it beautiful! What a perfect place to stop."

He looked around at her in surprise. "It's too soon to stop." He pointed to the other side. "Look how the terrain is changing. We're getting into the foothills. If we keep moving we should be out of this stuff before dark. I'd certainly appreciate a drier climate." He wiped the perspiration from his brow.

"Oh, but Wolf! Here's the perfect place to bathe. You said we would look for a place . . . and you found one."

"Dammit, Kelly. I was only humoring you. I didn't expect to actually find one."

She smiled at him. "But you did." He greeted her smile with a deeper frown. "Aw, c'mon, Wolf. It'll only take a few minutes.'' She quickly shucked off the knapsack, found the bar of soap and immediately sat down to pull off her shoes.

''Kelly—''

''I won't be but a minute. I promise.'' As unselfconscious as if she were alone, Kelly peeled off her shirt and stepped out of her slacks. Grabbing the bar of soap she began to walk gingerly to the edge of the water.

''Be careful. You have no idea how deep it is there.''

She glanced over her shoulder. ''I'm a good swimmer, though.''

So much for being in charge of this expedition, Wolf thought with irritation. What the hell was he standing there for? If she got into trouble he'd have to jump in and save her, and he sure as hell didn't want to get everything he owned wet! He removed the backpack, sat down and jerked off his shoes.

When he looked up he discovered that she was fine. She'd waded out to the middle of the pool. The water was chest high, and the spray from the waterfall was as good as any shower. Because of the roar of the water he couldn't hear her, but he understood her motion to join her in the water.

Since it didn't look as though they were going anywhere for the moment, he might as well make the most of it. The truth was, he was already hot and sweaty from swinging the machete. The water would feel good. He stripped out of all but his briefs, then eased himself into the pool.

Kelly immediately joined him, handing him the soap and pantomiming that he could scrub her back! Before he could tell her no, she had turned away, leaving him holding the slippery soap. Resigned to the inevitable, he began to smooth the soap along her back. Here in the shallows, the water came to her mid-thighs. The wet underwear no longer protected her from his view.

He closed his eyes and tried to think of something else. He'd been without a woman for too long, that was all. It wasn't that he was reacting to her personally, he reminded himself. He didn't think he was buying that one, however.

She reached up and unfastened her hair, then ducked her head under water, turning her delectable derriere up an arm's length in front of him. What the hell did she think he was, anyway, some sort of eunuch?

When she turned around she took the soap from his hand. He made no attempt to resist. Instead, he headed toward the deepest part of the pool where the water was falling the hardest and stayed there until his body and his mind cooled down.

He'd been thinking ever since they broke camp about what he could do to camouflage her skin and hair coloring. There were berries that would stain, if he could just remember what they looked like.

By the time he'd soaped himself down, rinsed off and gotten out, he knew what he was going to do.

Kelly watched him after he got out of the water. He didn't seem to be in a hurry to leave. In fact, he was ignoring her completely. He was gathering something off the low-lying bushes that grew beside the water.

She tried to call to him several times but he couldn't hear her.

Didn't he ever play? Did he even know how? He had gotten into the water, swum ferociously, washed and gotten out. Now he was busy mixing something together.

Her curiosity finally got the best of Kelly. She got out of the water and dried off. She was just starting to dress when he touched her shoulder. She jumped.

"You scared me!" She had to yell over the noise of the falls.

"Sorry. Before you get dressed, I want you to rub this on your arms, legs and face."

She looked at the unappetizing mudlike substance with something akin to horror. "Are you serious?"

"Yes. It will stain your skin."

"But I don't want my skin stained. I like it just the way it is."

"Too bad." He stared at her for a moment, then deliberately stuck two fingers in the mixture, then smeared them across her nose and cheeks. Although she yelped, she didn't move away. "It won't be so bad. You only have to leave it on for fifteen minutes or so, then wash off the residue."

While he worked on her face, she timidly stuck her fingers in it. "Yuck. That feels slimy."

"It doesn't matter how it feels. It's how it's going to look that's important."

She smeared the mixture on her arms, then down her legs. After he finished her face, he started working on her neck and shoulders. "Whoa, wait a minute," she said, taking a step back. "I don't have to wear this all over, do I?"

"No," he replied patiently, "but since you wear your shirts open at the neck, you're going to have to be the same color wherever you're seen."

"Oh." She looked down at herself and shuddered. "I don't feel like I've even had a bath."

"Too bad."

"Why aren't you wearing something like this?"

"Because I'm dark enough. I could easily pass for a native in this country. You're the one who looks out of place."

She sighed, waiting for the prescribed time to elapse. When she felt him touch her hair, she whirled away from him. "Not my hair!"

"Yes. Until I can find something to make it look darker, this will at least cover most of the red."

"It will *ruin* it!"

"Okay."

"A lot you care."

"You got that right."

"You're making me look so ugly!" she wailed, catching a glimpse of her reflection in the water.

Actually, she looked like a little girl who had been caught playing in the mud, or so Wolf tried to convince himself. Her flesh-colored briefs and bra still clung to her like a second skin. There was no way she could be mistaken for a child looking like that. But her eyes had rounded and her bottom lip appeared on the verge of quivering.

Kelly looked as though she were going to cry.

Wolf felt like a heel. She'd been in such a good mood all morning, as though their situation was more of a lark than a threat to their lives. She had played in the water, laughing and splashing, trying to splash him.

Well, he'd certainly managed to ruin her mood.

Without changing his expression, he said, "Go ahead and wash it off, now. Let's see how well it does."

When she got out, she *was* crying. Her skin had a gray, doughy look to it. Her hair no longer sparkled in the sunlight, but was a nondescript color that wouldn't catch the eye.

Okay, so she hated him now. Maybe it was just as well. The new coloring might end up saving her life. He wouldn't have done it if he hadn't felt it necessary, but he wasn't about to explain his actions to her.

He didn't care what she thought of him. Maybe now she wouldn't be so damned talkative.

Eight

"Wolf?"

"Hmm."

"Are you asleep?"

"Yes."

"Will you talk to me?"

"No. Go to sleep."

Kelly lay beside Wolf on the sleeping bag, the blanket pulled up to her neck. After they had left the waterfall that morning, they had climbed steadily. Although they were still in the jungle, it had a different feel to it. It wasn't so close, so smothering and damp. In fact, the blanket felt good tonight. So did Wolf's body heat coming from only a few inches away.

"I can't sleep," she finally explained to the darkness.

"Fake it."

"I've been faking it for hours. It doesn't work."

"I don't intend to sing you to sleep, Kelly. So shut up and go to sleep."

She chuckled at the thought of Wolf singing, then her smile slowly faded. Why was he such a grouch? He never lightened up. After all, they had gotten away, hadn't they? There was no evidence that anyone had followed them. So why was he so grumpy?

He never talked. In fact, he acted as though he were alone. The only time he spoke was to give her orders, and even that was rare. She watched and learned from him, so that by the time they stopped to camp, she'd been able to help with the tent and bedroll.

He hadn't even said, "Thank you for your help."

No matter how friendly she tried to be, he ignored her.

He really was irritating, exasperating and more than a little arrogant. So why did she like him so much? Because he was so much more. He watched out for her, and he set his pace with her stamina in mind. He had insisted on checking her for bites and blisters each day, rubbing cream into any place that might become infected. He was thoughtful and caring.

But he was still a grump and a grouch.

"Wolf?"

Silence.

"Why are you such a grouch?"

More silence.

"Was it something you developed as you grew up or did you inherit it?"

"Inherited it," he muttered.

She smiled in the darkness. She had known all along he wasn't asleep. He had lain too still and breathed too shallowly.

"From whom?"

"My grandfather."

"It's hard for me to picture you with a family. You seem so independent. I guess I figured that you were born in a cave somewhere with a litter of wolf pups and just came down out of the mountains for your education."

"You've got a wild imagination."

"So where *were* you born?"

"On a ranch near the Guadalupe Mountains in West Texas."

"Did you have any brothers?"

"No."

"Did you have any sisters?"

"No."

"Just a mother and father, huh?"

"No."

She turned and peered at him through the darkness. "No? What kind of answer is that?"

"The truth."

"C'mon, Wolf. Talk to me. Tell me about being born on a ranch without a mother or father and inheriting your grandfather's grouchiness."

He was quiet for several minutes and Kelly had just about decided to give up when he said, "If I tell you the damned story of my life will you for God's sake shut up and go to sleep?"

She bit her bottom lip to keep from chuckling. "Yes," she said in a very small voice.

Silence reigned once more in the small tent but this time Kelly waited patiently. Another thing she had learned about Wolf was that he kept his word.

So she waited.

"My mother was a college student in Albuquerque, New Mexico, the summer she met my dad. She'd been raised on an Apache reservation in northwest New Mexico. She had always wanted to be a nurse and had finally talked her father into allowing her to move away from home so that she could go to school."

Kelly almost held her breath, so afraid was she to make the slightest move that would disrupt his story.

"Her name was Running Deer and she was beautiful," he said in a low voice. After a moment, he went on. "My dad was following the rodeo circuit, and he'd already made a name for himself by the time he saw my mother. Not all of his reputation was made in the arena, but my mother was too innocent to understand who and what he was."

She could hear the bitterness in his voice but said nothing to disturb his memories.

"I always wondered why he married her. I don't guess anybody will ever know. But by the time the rodeo was over Gilbert Conroe, Junior, had married Running Deer. He carried her off to West Texas to the ranch my grandfather owned."

A thin thread of pain was working its way into his voice and he cleared his throat. "Gil Senior was less than impressed with his son's choice of a wife. I understand he was livid. It didn't matter that she was beautiful, and kind, and loving, as well as intelligent. She was an Apache. That's all he could see.

"They had been at the ranch less than a month when Running Deer woke up one morning to find Gil Junior gone. He'd taken off to another rodeo, leaving her behind. Nobody knew when he would be back. He'd told Running Deer that she could finish her education and become a nurse, but they were miles away from any college.

"She began to do the cooking for my grandfather. When the cook for the men got drunk one time too many, Gil Senior fired him, so Running Deer cooked for everyone, which meant she was in the kitchen by four o'clock in the morning to have breakfast ready for the men when they rolled out of bed."

Kelly thought that Wolf told the story as though he'd been there witnessing it as it happened. She wondered how he knew, but wouldn't ask . . . at least, not at the moment.

"After two months Running Deer decided to go back to New Mexico. Her father-in-law treated her like an unpaid servant, and she hadn't heard anything from Gil Junior." He stopped talking for a long time and Kelly decided that he wasn't going to tell her anything more. She hated having the story stop in the middle like that. Did Running Deer go home? Did her husband come back? Where did Wolf fit into the story?

He shifted, as though trying to find a more comfortable position. "It was about that time that Running Deer realized she was pregnant . . . with me. She was trapped."

Kelly made a noise of disbelief and possible argument, but he ignored her. "So she did what she had to do. She stayed and looked after my grandfather. After I was born, she looked after me. She kept the house, cooked the meals, did the laundry. My grandfather did his best to ignore her."

"What about your father?" she whispered.

"Oh, he showed up from time to time. He said he had intended to take her with him but he wasn't going to haul a kid around." His voice had grown harsher.

"Do you blame yourself for your mother's unhappiness?"

After a long silence, he sighed and said, "No. No, I don't. My mother loved me with every fiber of her being. She felt that I was her whole reason for living."

"Did she ever go back to school?"

"No. I remember one time we took a bus and traveled all the way to northern New Mexico to see her people. I must have been around five or six. I don't know, exactly. I just remember her excitement and her eagerness for me to meet her family."

"What happened?"

"They were cool and distant to both of us. I guess I looked too much like my dad for them to accept me, which was ironic, since my grandfather used to complain that his only grandson looked like a damned Apache."

"Where is your mother now?" she asked after a moment.

"She died when I was seven."

"Oh, Wolf! No! How did she die?"

"The doctor said it was pneumonia. She collapsed one morning while preparing breakfast. The doctor said that she was run down and that she'd probably been sick for a while before that. By the time he got there, there was nothing for him to do. She died late that night."

"Oh, Wolf," she whispered, tears pouring down her face. She felt that she knew Running Deer, knew her pain and her fear, knew her joy in her son, her hope for his future. Kelly felt as though she'd just received word that a very good friend had died. "What did you do after that?"

"Went to school, mostly. That and worked on the ranch. That's when I started going up into the mountains. Jake, my grandfather's foreman, sorta adopted me. I learned most of my personal history from him. He'd known my dad since Gil Junior was a kid. He kept hoping that Dad would settle down and come home. Once Running Deer died, he never came back."

"Not even to see you?"

"No. He had a fight with my grandfather during his last visit. I don't know for sure, but I would guess it had to do with him staying there and helping with the ranch and raising me. I heard their angry voices one night. The next morning he was gone."

"So your grandfather raised you."

"In his fashion."

"Whatever happened to him?"

"He died when I was overseas. By the time I heard the news, they'd already buried him. He left everything he had to me. I told the lawyers to sell it all and bank it. When I got out of the marines I took the money and headed east to get educated." After a mo-

ment he growled, "So now you have my life story. Go
to sleep."

"Thank you for telling me, Wolf," she whispered,
still fighting the tears.

"Don't thank me. Just let me get some sleep."

Kelly lay there thinking of all that Wolf had told her.
No wonder he wouldn't allow anyone to get close to
him. Why should he?

She was glad that he'd made friends with Sam. Sam
was such an extrovert. He had befriended Wolf, much
as she hoped to do. She was encouraged by Sam's
success. It gave her hope.

Kelly rolled over and tucked herself against the
warmth of Wolf's back.

Damn the woman, anyway, Wolf thought, lying
there wide awake. How the hell did she expect him to
sleep with her full, warm breasts pressed tightly
against his back? Maybe they'd have to do something
about the sleeping arrangements. Maybe he'd give her
the sleeping bag to herself tomorrow night. He could
make do with the blanket.

How in the hell had she talked him into telling her
about his family? Nobody besides Sam knew about his
past.

Sam had been with him when he'd gotten the news
about his grandfather. He'd sat with him for hours
while Wolf had tried to feel something for the man
who had left him everything he'd ever worked for in
his life. The pain came from realizing that he couldn't
feel much of anything for the man. As a kid, he'd
stayed out of his way as much as possible. He'd been
a real grouch, the old man. Yeah. That was what had

started the conversation. Kelly had called him a grouch. So maybe he was more like the old man than he'd ever thought.

Now that he was older he could better understand what had happened all those years ago, but he still remembered his bewilderment as a child. Nobody seemed to like him. He was neither one thing nor another. He was a mixture that nobody wanted. He had tried to please his grandfather, but could never remember hearing a word of praise from the old man.

Would it have made a difference? Wolf didn't know. How could he possibly know what it would feel like to have been raised by a father and mother who loved him? What would it have felt like to have had his grandfather proud of him? He had no idea.

But he was never going to do that to a child. At least he knew he didn't have the knowledge or the wisdom to be a father. He would never put a child through what he had gone through.

Sam could joke about his getting married someday, but both of them knew that it would never happen. He had chosen his life, and his life-style. He was well and truly content with what he had made of his life. Even if he never made it back from their present situation, he knew that he had accomplished everything he had wanted to accomplish.

He'd started a scholarship fund for children from the reservation who couldn't afford to go to college without financial assistance. He'd made certain that Jake received enough retirement income to be comfortable for the rest of his life. He'd gotten a card from Jake the previous Christmas, pointing out that he was just too cantankerous to die and inviting Wolf to visit him the next time he was in Arizona.

Wolf had no regrets. He'd done what he could. He'd accepted what he couldn't change about his life. And he'd gone forward.

But if he ever got back to the States, he was going to let Sam know in no uncertain terms that he would never, ever let him talk him into anything else as long as they both lived! Without Sam's interference Wolf would be camped out right now in the high valley of the Guadalupes, staring at the stars, which seemed especially large over Texas.

Instead, he had a beautiful woman curled up to his back, driving him more than half out of his mind with desire, while he plotted ways to keep them both alive until he could deliver her to her parents.

God only knew if he could handle this latest challenge.

"Oh, Wolf, look!"

Wolf spun around, his heart pounding, only to find that Kelly was pointing to something off in the distance. She was not threatened by some deadly predator.

Taking a deep breath, he tried to slow his heartbeat and stop the adrenaline rush that had hit him as soon as he heard her excited voice.

"What is it?" he asked in what he considered a calm, rational voice.

She frowned at him in exasperation. "Oh, Wolf, for heaven's sake. Lighten up, will you? Didn't you even notice?" She pointed again. "This is the first time we've been able to see where we've been. Isn't the view breathtaking?''

Wolf looked around and admitted that the view was, indeed, spectacular. He had discovered a path that morning that had made their journey considerably easier. It looked as though it was used by animals and people alike. He no longer needed to forge a trail, which had encouraged him to think that the most difficult part of their journey was over.

Kelly was right. There was no reason they couldn't stop and enjoy the view.

''Have you ever seen anything like it?''

''Not recently, no.''

''Is this what it looks like in West Texas?''

Wolf laughed. ''Hardly. Too much greenery for West Texas.''

Kelly could scarcely believe it. Wolf had laughed! She hadn't heard him laugh since the night they had escaped. Kelly no longer cared why he was laughing. It could be at her, for all she cared.

''Is that where we're headed?'' she asked, pointing to even higher mountains.

''Yes.''

She shook her head. ''Who would have believed it?''

''Believed what?''

''That I would be hiking in the mountains. I've never been much for outdoor activities.''

He chuckled, his grin warming her even more. ''I would have never guessed,'' he replied.

She swatted at his shoulder. "Just because I've never done it before doesn't mean I'm not enjoying myself."

His eyes narrowed in surprise. "You are?"

"Sure. Aren't you?"

He stared at the top of her head, where a dirty bandanna covered her hair, to her stained face, down to the rumpled shirt that hung shapelessly over a pair of wrinkled baggy pants and stopped at the toes of her scuffed sneakers.

In no way did this woman resemble the immaculately turned out sister of the bride he'd met little over a week ago. "If your friends could only see you now."

His white smile slashed across the darkness of his face, while his eyes glittered with amusement. Kelly stood staring at him, mesmerized by the relaxed enjoyment he projected.

I love this man, she finally admitted to herself. Of course she did. She felt as though she had always loved him, wanted to hold and caress him, wanted to smooth away his pain.

"Kelly?"

"Hmm?"

"What's wrong?"

"What?"

"What's wrong with you? You look as though you've gone into some kind of trance."

"Oh!" She attempted a natural-sounding laugh. "I guess I was visualizing the faces of everyone at the office if I could send them a snapshot of me at the moment."

"Don't worry. They'd never recognize you."

Once again, she turned to look at the awesome splendor of their surroundings. "I can better understand why you're so interested in taking care of the planet. This is all so beautiful. I wish I had a camera."

He shook his head. "Somehow, that doesn't surprise me in the least. I'm certain it would have been one more necessity you would have insisted on packing."

He was teasing her!

"I wish I'd packed some detergent. Everything we have with us is filthy. When are we going to find a laundromat around here?"

He studied the terrain for some time before saying, "I would guess that there's a runoff over in that area. At least we could stop and bathe and wash a few of our things, if you want."

"Oh, Wolf, that sounds wonderful!" She threw her arms around his neck and kissed him.

He stiffened with shock and jerked his mouth away from hers. "What the hell was that for?"

"I was just thanking you for being so considerate of my wishes." She kept her hands hooked securely together around his neck, so that she was pressed against him from chest to thigh.

"What makes you think I'm being so considerate of you? I'd like to get clean as much as you would." He seemed to be having trouble knowing what to do with his hands. He'd rested them on her shoulders, then restlessly moved them up and down her back.

Kelly went up on tiptoe and pressed her lips against his once again, flicking her tongue across his mouth.

His arms tightened around her and she sighed, loving the feel of him against her. She could feel his heart thudding against her chest.

What the hell did she think she was doing? Wolf intended to push her away, to let her know in no uncertain terms that— But, oh, she tasted so good, and she felt even better pressed up against him like that. She was making that little sound in her throat, a sort of purring that drove him wild.

The kiss went on and on as neither one wanted to be the first to end it. Wolf slipped his hand beneath her shirt and quickly discovered that she wasn't wearing a bra. He cupped one of her breasts and brushed his thumb across the peak, feeling it harden. How was he supposed to resist this woman? He ached for her.

Eventually she pulled away from him, gasping for air. She rested her head on his shoulder and held him as tightly as she could. Never had any man affected her so strongly. She wanted him. She wanted him now, next week, next month, next year. She wanted to be there when he walked into the house each day. She wanted to provide him with the warmth of a loving home. She wanted to have his children, to allow him to experience the miracle of producing such perfect little beings from the wonder of their love.

At the moment, she contented herself with stroking the nape of his neck, while she placed tiny kisses just under his chin.

"This is insane," he said after a moment. She smiled. He seemed to be having trouble finding his voice.

"Is it?"

"Of course it is. It's just because we've been forced into a situation that's so unusual, so..."

"Otherwise, you wouldn't be attracted to me at all, is that what you're saying?"

"Yes. I mean, no, of course not. I've always found you attractive. It's just that—" He reached behind his neck and took her hands, forcing them down and away from him. He took a careful step away from her so that their bodies no longer touched. He continued to hold her wrists, as though afraid of what she might do if she were free to move.

He tried again. "It's just that—we couldn't be more opposite. We absolutely have nothing in common. You've always lived in cities. I prefer the wilderness. You've got your own interests that are very different from mine."

"Okay."

He had been about to say something else, but her easy agreement stopped him with his mouth open. "Okay? What's that supposed to mean?"

"It means that I understand that you might be afraid of me."

"Afraid of you! Now, that's a laugh! I may be afraid of a great many things, but you aren't one of them."

She crossed her arms and looked at him. "I happen to think you are. You're scared to death at the thought that you might fall in love with me, want to marry me, want to have a family with me."

"Are you out of your mind? You've got a wild imagination. I already knew that. But what in the hell are you carrying on about now?"

She looked past his shoulder. "If we're going to find some water, we'd better get going, don't you think?"

"Don't change the subject."

"I'm not. I say you're afraid of me. You say you're not. Since we're both entitled to our own opinions, I would assume that our discussion is now at an end. I'm obviously not going to be able to convince you that you're afraid of me. By the same token, there's no way you're going to be able to convince me you're not." She pulled the bandanna off her head, smoothed her hair back, then carefully tied the piece of material back in place. She patted his arm and said cheerfully, "Shall we go?"

Nine

The woman was crazy, that was the problem, Wolf decided as he trudged up the winding path. The strain of their situation had been too much for her. She'd gone over the edge. So she'd come up with some fixation on him. It didn't mean anything. He'd just ignore her fantasies, and once they reached the embassy she would see why he had treated her theories with the amusement they deserved.

The problem was, Wolf was far from amused. The kiss they had shared had pushed him almost to the breaking point. It didn't matter to him that she wasn't dressed in the latest fashion. He knew very well what was under those shapeless clothes she wore. How could he forget what she had looked like in her wet and clinging underwear? She might as well have been nude. How many times had he awakened and realized that he'd been dreaming about her slowly coming out of the water to him.

If the only attraction he felt for her had been physical Wolf knew that he could have handled it better. The problem was that he liked Kelly Corcoran. Actually, he admired her very much. She wasn't the spoiled brat he'd first thought she was. She had kept her head during some very traumatic experiences. She'd had to adapt, and few people could have adapted with the style and good humor that Kelly had shown. He liked that in a person. He really did.

He found himself thinking about how much he'd like to take her into the Guadalupes with him. He knew that she would appreciate the beauty there. He could just imagine her excitement at seeing the deer grazing, or maybe they would spot a cougar or watch the eagles soar high overhead.

Wolf had never before had the desire to share that private world with another person. It would never have occurred to him that he would want to share it with a woman.

She'd been wrong. He wasn't afraid of her. He just had a very healthy desire to guard his own independence. Just because he had no intention of giving it up for Kelly, or anyone else, for that matter, did not mean he was afraid. He resented her suggesting such a thing.

They heard the trickle of the water more and more clearly as they climbed higher. Wolf had left the path but had carefully marked the way they had come. They would return to the path after they had bathed, washed some clothes and rested. He had only a few more days' supply of food. He hoped they would come across a mountain village and do some bartering.

They came upon the small, grassy glade unexpectedly. One moment they were climbing, mostly on hands and knees, the next moment they were able to stand and look upon a scene of fairy-tale wonder.

"Oh, Wolf," Kelly whispered in awe.

He knew what she meant.

A part of the mountain had fallen eons ago, forming perpendicular bluffs where water trickled down. A hollow semicircle of almost flat ground lay at the base of the bluffs. Massive rocks formed a barrier along the outer edge, effectively camouflaging what lay behind them. Thick grass grew beside a pondlike area, where the water flowed and eventually continued down the mountainside in a steady stream.

"I've never seen anything like it," Kelly said reverently. "Have you?"

"Not exactly, although there's a small valley high in the Guadalupe Mountains that this reminds me of. It's my favorite place to camp."

She glanced at him, her eyes shining. "How can you force yourself to leave it?"

Wolf knew that she had just dealt him an emotional blow from which he might never be able to recover. She understood! She knew why he continued to retreat to the mountains year after year. She understood why it was so difficult for him to return to the civilized world.

For the first time in his life, Wolf felt true empathy with another person. He was no longer alone.

He watched Kelly as she slipped her knapsack off and carried it over to the pool. There was plenty of sunlight, soft grass, water, even firewood. Although it was scarcely past noon, there was no reason not to set up camp. They would need to let the sun dry their clothes.

Without saying anything, Wolf found a place to set up their tent and went to work. Kelly pulled out her other clothes and took off her shoes and socks, then the pants she was wearing. The shapeless shirt she wore barely reached her thighs.

Wolf laid out the clothes he needed to wash, as well as food. He did his best to ignore her by gathering firewood and spreading the bedroll in the tent.

By the time he had the food ready, she had spread her newly washed clothes out to dry.

"It's a good thing that bar of soap was bath size," she said with a grin, sitting down beside the fire. "Otherwise, we'd be in big trouble."

Wolf knew he was already in big trouble as soon as she approached. Her long bare legs were like magnets to his eyes. He concentrated on his food without glancing up again.

"Wolf?"

"Hmm?"

"Would you like me to wash your clothes?"

"I'll do it."

"I don't mind."

"I said I'd do it."

"Okay, okay...grouch." She sounded as though she was smiling, but he didn't look up to see. "I think I'll take a bath after I get through eating." She waited to see if he was going to comment. When he didn't, she went on. "Do you have any idea how far we've come?"

"No."

"Or how much farther it is to Bogotá?"

"No."

"Gee, Wolf. You're such a fount of information. Sometimes I'm overwhelmed by it all."

"Has anyone ever told you that you talk too much?"

She closed her eyes to better consider the question. "Nope. I can't remember anyone ever suggesting that."

He made a sound in his throat that was something like a growl. So what else was new? She had difficulty at times visualizing Wolf teaching. Maybe he showed lots of films, or handed out graphs, or even—she almost laughed out loud at the thought—maybe he recorded all the instructions he needed to give his classes at the beginning of each year, then played them at the appropriate times.

She wondered what he did when he was asked questions. Maybe he wrote the answers on the blackboard, or told them to look it up, or made that disgusted sound in his throat.

"What's so amusing?"

She looked at him. "Were you by chance talking to me?" she asked in exaggerated surprise.

"Why were you grinning like that?"

"Just thinking."

"About what?"

"You."

He glared at her. "Somehow I figured that. So what do you find so amusing about me?"

"I was trying to figure out how you taught school, since you don't like to talk."

"I enjoy teaching. I enjoy my subject. There's so much to cover I generally find myself getting too enthusiastic about the subject and talking too long."

"I'd love to see that," she murmured.

"I suppose you find me very boring."

"Not at all. I find you fascinating."

"Sure you do."

"No, really. You're such a contradiction. You try to be so rough and gruff on the outside, and yet you're really very tender and caring on the inside."

"What a bunch of nonsense!"

"How do you see yourself?"

"I don't bother looking."

"I bet you picture yourself as lean, mean, hard and tough."

"Is that the way you see me?"

"Sometimes."

"But not all the time?"

She shook her head. "I think you'd like people to think that you have no feelings, that you don't care about anything or anybody."

"That's not true. I care passionately about the helpless animals that are losing their homes because civilization is crowding them out of their natural habitat. I'm deeply concerned that if we don't start taking better care of our planet, it will die. I want a place for future generations to enjoy."

"Just not yours."

"What do you mean?"

"Any future generations will not come from you."

"There will be plenty of others, believe me."

"But haven't you ever thought about teaching your sons and daughters about the wilderness and the planet? Haven't you wanted to share your love for all of these things with your children so that they can grow up to carry on your work?"

"That's why I teach. I don't have to produce a person biologically in order to teach him or her."

"That's true. I suppose you'd have to get too close to a child of your own. You'd have to love it and be aware of its vulnerability and your own. I can see why the whole idea would be too much for you."

Wolf came to his feet and whirled away from her, taking several steps before coming to a halt. "I thought you wanted to go take a bath."

Kelly stood up. "Great idea. Glad you reminded me." She walked away from their camp, unbuttoning her shirt.

Wolf had to get away from there. Damn, the woman could irritate him quicker than anyone he'd ever known. Who in hell did she think she was with her dime-store analysis of him? Who asked her to take him apart and examine all the pieces? He was doing fine, thank you very much. He certainly didn't need her to help him deal with his life.

By the time he returned, almost an hour had passed. He glanced around to make certain she was all right, but he didn't see her at first. He frowned, then peeked into the tent. It was empty.

He started toward the pond, then spotted her. He froze in his steps. She had bathed, all right. All the stain had disappeared. She was stretched out on the far side of the pond on their blanket, sound asleep.

She wore only her shining, flame-red hair for cover. She lay on her stomach, her hand tucked under her cheek, facing him, but her eyes were closed. She'd spread her hair to dry, and it fell in waves across her shoulders and back. His gaze traveled down her back to her waist, then up over the provocative swell of her buttocks, down her thighs to her knees, her calves and down to her slim ankles and feet. No one had ever looked more beautiful, more perfect, to him.

Wolf went over and picked up the pile of clothes he'd pulled out of the backpack earlier. Like Kelly, who had decided to wash everything she owned, he needed to do the same thing.

He stripped down to his briefs, then carried the clothes to the water, where she had left the soap lying on a rock. He began to scrub, forcing his mind to remain blank, refusing to look at the woman across from him.

However, his resistance had worn thin. How much was one man supposed to take?

After getting everything as clean as he could, Wolf stepped out of his briefs and scrubbed them, as well. Then he grabbed the soap and waded out to the middle of the pond.

The water on top was warm, but the deeper it got, the more aware Wolf became that the water was runoff from the mountains. He stopped when the water level reached his waist, then sank below the surface for as long as he could tolerate the temperature. It was the best substitute for a cold shower around, and he needed all the help he could get.

When he came up he used the soap to lather his hair and body. It felt good to do more than spot wash. Once again, Kelly had been right. He dunked himself to rinse off, and as he came up, his eyes still closed, something brushed against his arm. His eyes flew open and he discovered that Kelly had joined him in the water. Her hair had brushed against him.

"Hi! Isn't this great? I could swim in it all day."

The clear mountain water revealed that Kelly hadn't paused to put anything on before joining him in the water.

"I, uh, don't think this is such a good idea, Kelly," he managed to get out.

"You mean, swimming together?"

He nodded, trying to keep his eyes trained on her face.

She touched his cheek with her hand, brushing the drops of moisture away. "Don't you ever like to play?" she asked.

"Play?" The word sounded strangled in his throat.

"You know. Do something just for the fun of it. Do we have to be serious all the time? Can't we just relax and enjoy life?"

Wolf's control snapped. "All right," he growled, pulling her to him. "Let's enjoy life, then." His mouth came down on hers with bruising force.

She didn't fight him. Instead, he could have sworn he heard a chuckle in her throat as she wrapped her arms around his neck and her legs around his waist. She returned his kiss with enthusiasm.

With her legs around him, Kelly was pressed intimately against him, so that he was only a short distance away from totally possessing her. That seemed to be Wolf's last coherent thought.

He began to walk toward the edge of the pond, his hands locked together under her hips, his mouth devouring hers. They came out beside the blanket where she'd been lying earlier.

He was on fire, and she appeared to feel the same. Her hands touched him all over—his chest, his back, his hip—when he knelt on the blanket and began to lower her onto her back. She clutched at him tightly, refusing to let go.

It no longer mattered. Nothing mattered at the moment except possessing this woman—this tantalizing, teasing, utterly irresistible woman.

She shifted, touching him, guiding him to enter her. He tried to pull back . . . they were going too fast. He needed to slow down, to take it easy, to—ahhhh!

She was so tight, he could hardly move. He attempted to pull away. He didn't want to hurt her. He wanted this to be good for her. She followed his movement, encasing him smoothly in an upward surge.

Wolf went up in flames.

She felt like molten lava surging all around him, squeezing and releasing, moving against him. She was engulfing him, devouring him, turning him into an inferno of need.

Wolf exploded, or so it felt to him. His body seemed to become a part of her. He held her tightly in a convulsive attempt to hang on to something, to anything, in order not to lose himself forever in the myriad sensations that had taken control of him.

When Wolf finally became aware of anything, he realized that he was still sprawled across Kelly. They were both gasping for air. He was probably smothering her. He knew he needed to move but his body felt incapable of moving.

He tried to find the words, or the thoughts, that could express what had just happened to him. But it was no use.

He forced his forearms to hold his weight and raised himself slightly off her. Her face was framed by his arms, and she gazed at him as though she'd just seen paradise. He closed his eyes, unable to face the blinding radiance that shone in her expression.

He started to slide off her, but she clamped her legs tighter, holding him to her, very much inside of her. "Don't move," she whispered. "Please."

"I'm too heavy," he finally managed to say between gasps.

She just shook her head. They continued to lie there for several moments in silence. Wolf expected his body to recognize its cataclysmic fulfillment and relax somewhat. It didn't.

He rested his forehead against hers and she took the opportunity to kiss him, her lips warm and swollen. She kissed his nose, his eyelids. She kissed him wherever she could reach, as though she were hungry for him.

Wolf lowered himself to his side, pulling her with him, then rolled to his back. Her knees rested on either side of his hips. She lifted her body slightly, then slowly lowered herself upon him.

He groaned.

"Did that hurt?"

He shook his head.

She did it again, leaning forward slightly so that her breasts touched his chin. He lowered his head and pulled one of the delicate nipples into his mouth, giving it a gentle tug.

This time it was Kelly who groaned.

"Did that hurt?" he asked, pulling away.

She shook her head, so he did it again. She began to move her hips in the same rhythm he used to tug at her breasts, as though they were well rehearsed in the art of making love to each other.

This time was slower as each of them explored the other. Kelly sat back so she could see his chest, touching and exploring the wide shoulders, the developed pectoral muscles. He felt as though he were tactilely memorizing her as he ran his hands along her ribs, down to her waist, out over the swell of her hips, then inward to where they fit so perfectly together. Then upward until he held each breast in his hands, weighing them, stroking them, eventually coaxing them down to where his mouth could find them once more.

When he could no longer ignore the inner pressure and tension he slid his hands to her hips and took control of her movements. He met her, thrust for thrust, until she cried out her release and he could feel the contractions pulling at him, forcing him to let go and give in to that life-giving pressure, his body taking over completely as his mind went blank in the ecstasy of the moment.

They must have fallen asleep, for when Wolf next opened his eyes, the sun was far in the west. He glanced down at Kelly, asleep in his arms. She looked very peaceful with a slight smile on her lips, as though she were exactly where she wanted to be.

He frowned, remembering what had happened. He'd certainly lost control of himself. My God, he'd taken her with little to no thought about consequences.

There was time enough to face that later. They needed to get dressed and gather their clothes before dark.

"Kelly?"

"Hmm."

"We need to pick up our clothes before dark. Otherwise the dew will dampen them again."

Kelly lazily opened her eyes and smiled up at him with slightly swollen lips. "Must you always be so blasted practical?"

He grinned. "I think one of us needs to be."

She yawned. "I suppose." She sat up, looking around them. "If I had to try to imagine what paradise looks like, I'd have to picture this," she said, looking around her. Wolf stood up and she turned her gaze to him.

His tall, lean body radiated leashed energy and sexuality. It was all she could do to refrain from touching him as he stood there, the western sun touching his face and gilding his features.

He was magnificent. Who wouldn't be proud to be a part of this man's life? She could see him in a loincloth and moccasins, a wolf beside his leg, ready to do battle, if necessary, in order to survive.

He walked away from her to the other side of the pond, where their clothes were spread out in the sun. With a sigh, Kelly got up and draped the blanket modestly around her. When she reached his side, he glanced at her and scowled. "You're a little late with that, aren't you?"

"With what?"

"Covering your delectable body."

She grinned. "Do you think it's delectable?"

He muttered something and turned away. They gathered the clothes in silence and returned to their camp. Kelly picked out a clean set of clothing for herself and disappeared into the tent. Beside the pond, Wolf had pulled on a pair of briefs and pants. Now he found socks and a shirt.

By the time dinner was ready, the last light had disappeared. Kelly sat across the campfire from him, watching him eat, watching him stare into the fire. He ignored her completely.

"Wolf?"

He glanced up.

"It's all right, you know."

A frown creased his forehead.

"What we did earlier. It's all right to celebrate life together. It's okay to be human, with human needs and desires. I wanted you to make love to me."

"Somehow I managed to get that idea."

"Are you going to deny that you wanted to make love to me?"

"That would be ridiculous, under the circumstances."

"So what's wrong?"

"What we did was careless and irresponsible."

"You mean because we didn't use any form of birth control?"

"That's a damned good place to start!"

"Then let's talk about it."

"What is there to say?"

"Okay. Then *I'll* talk about it." She paused, gathering her thoughts. "My only other experience was very disappointing to me. It happened in college and I decided then and there that sex wasn't something I was interested in." She glanced at him. "Until I met you."

He groaned, thinking about his lack of control where she was concerned.

"I do know enough about my body's functions to know that this is a safe time of the month for me. I know what I'm doing, Wolf, and I take full responsibility for my actions."

"Why doesn't that make me feel any better?" Wolf muttered.

She studied him for a few moments before she asked, "So what else is bothering you?"

She waited for a long while before he raised his gaze from his intent study of the flames and said, "You. You bother me."

"In what way?"

"In every way. I don't want to get involved with you."

"You already *are* involved with me."

He rolled his eyes. "No kidding."

"No. I mean, you and I were involved as soon as we met. We got even more involved when we were kidnapped. Even if we hadn't made love, Wolf, we would still be involved. We've each made a vital impact on the other. We're not just going to be able to walk away from this time together and pretend that it never happened."

"I know."

"So why fight it?"

"It doesn't look as though we did."

"Oh, but you are. You've been pretending ever since we woke up earlier that I'm not here. That you didn't make love to me, and that you don't want me again."

He closed his eyes.

"Why don't we agree to enjoy the time we have together, to explore this beautiful country and build some wonderful memories to share with our children someday." She grinned and said. "Oops. I'll share them with *my* children. You can share them with your students, how's that?"

"So you're saying we should continue to sleep together until all this is over?"

"Wolf, we've been *sleeping* together every night since we left Boston. However, without the tension between us, I have a hunch we'll actually sleep, instead of finally passing out with exhaustion after hours of tossing and turning."

"You're really serious, aren't you? You don't intend to return to the States and announce our engagement."

"Are you kidding? Why would I want to be married to somebody who ignored me all the time? No thanks, Wolf."

"You think I ignore you?" he asked, disbelief evident in his voice.

"I know you do."

"I've been so damned aware of you these last few days that I've been out of my mind."

"You must make a great poker player because nobody could guess what you're thinking from the way you act."

He stared at her.

"I'm not trying to trap you, Wolf. Believe me. I'm enjoying being with you, more than I've ever enjoyed anything in my life. I want to make the most of the time we have together. Is there something wrong with that?"

Wolf stared at the woman who sat across the fire from him, enjoying the way the light flickered across her skin. She wasn't demanding a future from him. She wanted nothing more than what he was willing to give, for as long as he was willing.

He could handle that. Of course he could. It would also make the ensuing days and weeks easier to get through, knowing that he could go to sleep each night with her in his arms.

Without saying anything, he began to put out the fire. Kelly watched for a few moments in silence before she crawled into the tent and waited for her lone wolf to come to her.

Ten

The sound of heavy rain beating down on the tent aroused Wolf from a sound sleep. He and Kelly had managed to zip the sleeping bag around them so they were warm. Why shouldn't they be? He doubted that a knife blade could have been slipped between them anywhere.

He didn't like the sound of the rain. He fumbled for the zipper.

"What's the matter?" Kelly asked groggily.

"It's raining."

"That's nice." She rested her head on his chest.

"Not where we are at the moment, it isn't. We may have to move before we get washed away." He crawled out and began to dress. "You'd better get dressed, just in case."

The cool air swirled around her warm body as soon as Wolf moved away from her. Kelly sighed. Wouldn't you know? The first good night's sleep they had been able to enjoy and now the elements were against them.

She quickly dressed, pulled on her poncho, tied up her hair and began to roll up the sleeping bag

"Good girl," Wolf said a few minutes later, sticking his head into the tent. "We're going to have to move."

"Why doesn't that surprise me?" she murmured to herself, since he had immediately left. Because she trusted Wolf's instincts, that's why.

As soon as she crawled out, he began to pull down the tent. "I think I know of a spot where we can go until this blows over. I saw it on my walk this afternoon."

She was surprised that he had seen anything when he'd stomped off earlier in the day. As usual, she had made him furious. Somehow she had a real knack for doing that. Probably did him a lot of good. He intimidated most people.

She followed him when he led her around an outcropping and started up the mountain once more. She hated leaving their beautiful little spot, but perhaps there would be others.

They hadn't gone far when Wolf turned and lifted her onto a ledge. "Follow that around the corner, where it widens. There's a deep overhang there that should keep us dry."

Kelly followed his instructions and found a wide opening that seemed to lead back into the mountain.

As soon as Wolf joined her, he turned on the flashlight. "See? This will be perfect."

He was right. The ceiling was high enough so that they could stand up, and there was a place close to the opening where they could build a fire. All the comforts of home.

"Are you sure something else doesn't live here?"

"Yes. I checked it out earlier. In fact, I had thought about moving in here last night, but since we were already set up, I decided not to bother. I should have listened to my instincts."

"You mean you knew it would rain?"

"No. But I had a feeling that we needed to move and I didn't act on it."

"You get feelings like that often?"

"Often enough."

"Do you always listen?"

"Most of the time."

"When didn't you listen to your instincts?"

"When they kept telling me not to be best man at Sam's wedding!"

She began to laugh. "Poor Sam. You're never going to let him forget, are you."

"Not if I can help it."

He rolled out the sleeping bag and they both began to undress. "If you'd like, I could build a fire and make it warmer in here."

"This is all right."

"Maybe we should spread the sleeping bag out."

"Why? Is it too crowded for you to share?"

Wolf shrugged. "I was thinking about you."

She gave him a very seductive look. "I'm glad to hear it." She pulled off the remainder of her clothes and stretched out in the folds of the bag.

Wolf stripped down and crawled in beside her. "I remembered what you said."

"About what?"

"You didn't enjoy sex."

"I didn't until now. You've definitely made a convert out of me." She pulled him into her arms.

They made slow, leisurely love, caressing, exploring, teasing until they built up enough tension to create an explosion, then they fell asleep in each other's arms.

When Wolf woke up the next morning, the rain was still hurtling down. They wouldn't be going anywhere today. They would be confined to their shelter.

He recalled Kelly's words from the night before. She certainly showed no hint of aversion to his lovemaking. So what had he done, shown her the pleasures so that she could go on and enjoy them with someone else?

He didn't care for that idea very much. In fact, he didn't care for it at all, but there wasn't a damned thing he could do about it. After all, they had their own lives to lead. Once they returned to the States, there would be no reason to see each other again, unless Sam and Janet had them visit at the same time.

That wouldn't be a very good idea. He'd have to explain to Sam that— How, exactly, would he explain to Sam how it was between him and Kelly? Sam would probably give him a bad time, strongly suggest that he marry her—all of that nonsense.

If there was one thing Wolf knew for certain, it was that he wasn't ever going to get married. Of course, he could never imagine himself married to anyone but Kelly.

He lay there curled up around her body, holding her closely. He felt good. He felt complete. There was something very satisfying about knowing how much she trusted him. She had responded to him whole-heartedly, quickly learning how to please him, eager to show him how to please her. Her openness had touched him on a very fundamental level. He'd never felt so close to another person, never felt quite so safe.

It scared the hell out of him.

"Is it still raining?" she asked, gently wriggling against him.

"If you chose to open your eyes, you could check for yourself."

"'S too much trouble," she admitted.

"I guess we'll have to hike in the rain."

"Or we could stay here for the day," she pointed out.

"Won't that get boring?"

"I'd rather be dry and bored than soaking wet and trying to find our way across the mountains."

He hugged her to him. "I suppose I could devote my time and energy to seeing that you don't get *too* bored."

She turned her laughing face to him and said, "See how kind and considerate you are?" and gave him a smacking kiss.

The day generated a series of childish games and adolescent fantasies, all of which were thoroughly enjoyed by the participants.

Wolf paused and held up his hand to get her attention. She joined him and saw what had caused him to stop. About halfway down the mountain was a small village. More than a week had gone by since the rainy day they had spent playing in the cave. They were both dirty and hungry, and the village was a godsend.

Now that they were about to make connection with some form of civilization, Kelly could look back over the past week and better appreciate all that they had shared. However, when she'd awakened that morning knowing there was nothing more for them to eat and very little water, she had been concerned.

She and Wolf had drawn close during the past week. It was almost as though each knew what the other was thinking. Never one to talk much, Wolf had become even more quiet, but she no longer worried about his silence—not when he held her so close each night, loving her, allowing her to know his need for her.

It wasn't just his lovemaking that gave evidence of a change in him. It was also the way he watched her, the way he anticipated her needs, the way he would absently rub his hand across her shoulder or over her breast or hip in a light caress while studying the terrain around them. He seemed to draw as much comfort from touching her as she received from being touched.

"Do you want to stay here until I've talked with them?" he asked in a low voice.

She shook her head. He paid her the compliment of not questioning her decision. Instead, he took her hand and started down the path.

The people spoke an Indian dialect that Wolf could not understand, but he spoke to them in Spanish and they were able to understand him. So Wolf and Kelly were offered food, shown a place in which to bathe and given a place to sleep—in a room with another family.

The next morning they were waved on their way. As they continued traveling downhill, there were more and more people who could direct them on their way. Wolf couldn't believe their luck when they found someone with an ancient truck who agreed to drive them to Bogotá.

He was worried about Kelly. She'd become more and more quiet, her stamina almost gone, during the past week. She'd lost weight—they both had, due to their meager diet—and he was afraid she was going to become ill. She fell asleep in his arms as soon as they lay down each night, and he had trouble arousing her each morning. But she never uttered a word of complaint.

Their arrival in Bogotá was almost anticlimactic. No one gave them a second glance. They had taken the time to bathe and put on clean clothes, although everything they had with them was torn and wrinkled. Wolf had spent the evening before with Kelly seated in front of him, carefully combing the tangles from her hair.

"Have I ever told you how beautiful your hair is?"

She had glanced over her shoulder and had smiled at him shyly. "No, you never have."

"It reminds me of the flames that shoot up from our campfires."

"That sounds almost poetic."

"You make me feel like a poet sometimes."

She had leaned her head against his shoulder and closed her eyes. "I'm glad," she'd whispered on a sigh.

At the embassy they explained to the guard that they were United States citizens kidnapped from Boston and brought to Colombia. They got immediate attention.

Wolf insisted that the officials allow Kelly to get some rest and that he would answer any questions necessary. Instead, they were both fed and sent to bed after they gave one of the officials their names and told him who to contact to let Kelly's family know they were safe.

Wolf slept through the day and that night, waking up early the following morning. He stared out the window of his small room, trying to remember where he was and what he was doing there. Images flashed before his mind and he sat up, throwing off the covers.

Kelly!

Then he remembered. They were at the embassy. She was safe. They both were. Wolf sat on the side of the bed, trying to adjust to the fact that their ordeal was behind them. He felt disoriented, inside a room and sleeping on a bed. He'd been so tired when they'd shown him to his room that he had barely had the energy to shower before falling into bed.

He wanted to check on Kelly, to make certain she was all right. He looked at his backpack, dreading having to find something to wear, but it couldn't be helped.

A half hour later he was seated before Henry Pryor, one of the administrators.

"Well, Dr. Conroe, I must say you look considerably more rested than you did the last time I saw you. I know this whole unfortunate episode has been very grueling for you both."

"I haven't seen Kelly today. Do you know how she is?"

"Actually, we've had one of our doctors checking on her. She was running a fever when she came in, so we've been monitoring her."

"A fever! Why didn't somebody tell me?"

Henry smiled. "Because we didn't consider you in much better condition. Had you permitted it, we would have checked you, as well."

"Can I see her?"

"Of course. But if you don't mind, I'd appreciate your giving me some details regarding what happened to you. If you would describe the people, the places, anything that was said, that sort of thing, you will help us tremendously."

Wolf tried to curb his impatience. He knew the embassy officials needed as much information as possible. He certainly didn't want them bothering Kelly with questions. He was certain they were doing everything they could for her, but it didn't stop him from breaking out in a cold sweat, thinking about her being ill.

"Now then," Mr. Pryor said, turning on a recorder. "Why don't you get started by telling us what happened when you left the church after the wedding ceremony?"

Hours later, Wolf was shown to Kelly's room. He tapped on the door, and a woman in a white uniform opened it, saw him and smiled.

"You must be Dr. Conroe. Ms. Corcoran has been asking about you."

Wolf looked past the woman and saw Kelly sitting up in bed, looking at a book.

"Oh, Wolf! There you are. They won't let me out of bed. Isn't that ridiculous? I kept asking about you and they kept telling me you were all right, but—"

He walked over to the bed, already forgetting the woman who had opened the door and who now slipped out into the hallway. "As you can see, I'm doing all right."

She eyed the snug-fitting jeans, the Western shirt and unfamiliar shoes. "Where did you find the clothes?"

"Someone took pity on me and raided his closet. I was glad to find something else to wear." He sat on the bed, leaned over and kissed her lightly on the mouth. "What's this I hear about a fever?"

She shook her head, her hair falling over one shoulder. "The whole thing is ridiculous. So I'm a little feverish. It could be from the sunburn, or a low-grade infection, or..."

"So rest and take your medicine and you'll be fine."

She scowled at him. "That is *exactly* what the nurse keeps saying. Did you two rehearse together?"

"Just being practical."

She groaned.

"Have you eaten?"

"Enough for ten people. I think they bring a tray in every two hours."

"I must admit I'm enjoying the variety."

"Me, too."

They smiled at each other.

"Did you get in touch with your parents?"

She nodded. "I talked with them both this morning. They were still in shock over what had happened. They'd filed missing persons reports, called every authority they could think of to try to find us. When we weren't at the reception, nobody knew what to think. Finding out that we were kidnapped was quite a severe jolt." She smiled at him. "There had been some comment about the sparks between us, and Mother was concerned about how we managed to get along during our time together."

He took her hand and rubbed his thumb along the back of it. "Sparks?"

"Hmm. I know. I wasn't aware of any sparks."

"Me, either. I just knew you weren't too impressed with me."

"And you were less than impressed with me."

They stared into each other's eyes for a long moment without saying anything.

Finally Wolf spoke. "The ambassador said that he will personally see that we get home as soon as you feel like traveling."

"Good. I'm eager to get home."

Another long silence fell between them.

"Did you talk with Sam?"

"For a few minutes. Now that we've turned up safe and sound, he and Janet still intend to spend a week in the Virgin Islands for their honeymoon. Sam said they've spent the last few weeks hovering around the phone when they couldn't think of any other authority to contact."

"I understand my boss was highly concerned."

"Sam decided to tease me a little. Said he wouldn't have been surprised if I'd kidnapped you myself and taken you to the mountains with me."

"He did?"

"Uh-huh."

"Whatever would make him think something like that?"

He shrugged. "I heard him mutter something about sparks, but I didn't ask for an explanation." His gaze never left hers.

She touched his cheek, then ran her hand along his jawline. "So our great adventure has ended."

"Successfully, from all indications. I understand that our disappearance has been kept a secret and will continue to be just that. There's no reason to alert Santiago as to who he really kidnapped. The authorities intend to use the information we gave them to stop one avenue of drug smuggling, at least, through his contact in Boston."

"What do you intend to do now?"

"I'm not sure. I think I've done enough camping for a few weeks. I suppose I'll fly back to Albuquerque and enjoy the rest of my summer vacation. How about you?"

"I guess I'll go back to work and pick up the threads of my life. It will seem strange not to have Janet there, but I've had several months to get used to the idea. Who knows? I may advertise for another roommate."

"Just make sure that only females apply."

"Don't you believe in equal opportunity?"

"Let's just say that I'd like to meet any prospective roommate you might choose."

She looked at him, trying to read his expression. Once again, he was wearing his poker face.

"Why?"

He shrugged.

"Are you saying you don't want me to see anyone else?"

"No. I don't have the right to say anything about who you see or what you do."

"Do you want that right?"

He stood, moved away from the bed and walked over to the window.

"I guess I'm just being a little possessive, but I'll get over it. I've never spent so much uninterrupted time with anyone before. What we shared has nothing to do with who we are or with our real lives."

Kelly studied his broad back for a few moments before she said, "You don't think what happened between us was real?"

Wolf stood there for a moment, staring out the window, before he turned and looked at her. "No, Kelly, I don't. We were living out some kind of fantasy. What happened between us has nothing at all to do with real life."

Her smile was tender. "Whatever it was, I wouldn't have missed it for the world."

"Then you're not angry? You're not going to scream and rage at me for not suggesting we try to see each other?"

"No. You're the same man I met in Boston. I know that. You have your own life. I have mine. I'll always remember you with love. We shared some really beautiful times together."

"That's enough for you?" he asked intently.

Once again she smiled. "It has to be."

Eleven

***

Kelly let herself into her apartment, juggling the key, her purse and several letters she'd picked up downstairs. As soon as she was through the door, she tossed the key and her purse on a table and took the mail into the living room. Kicking off her shoes, she collapsed into one of the comfortable chairs and quickly flipped through the envelopes.

There was a fat letter from Janet, which she eagerly opened and scanned. It was full of daily happenings—filled with stories about Sam, househunting, her new position with the bureau, life in Durango, a visit to Albuquerque to see Wolf—

Wolf. There was his name written in her sister's familiar script. She began to read.

We finally decided to forget everything we had planned to do for the weekend and drive down to see Wolf in Albuquerque. What a beautiful drive that was! Kelly, I can hardly wait for you to come for a visit. Plan to stay for several weeks. It will take that long to show you around the area. There's so much to see— Mesa Verde National Park, the narrow-gauge train up to Silverton, the Million Dollar Highway, and that's just in Colorado alone!

Kelly looked up from the letter in exasperation. She mentioned going to visit Wolf then started a tourist's itinerary? Get on with it, Janet!

Sam has talked with Wolf several times since he got home, but this was the first time we'd seen him since you two were in Colombia. I must admit that I was shocked to see how much weight he'd lost. He looks grimmer, somehow, if that's possible. Not that he did much smiling before, you understand, but he was acting as though he'd lost his best friend.

Anyway, he did seem pleased to see us. Made us dinner, which really impressed me. The guy can really cook, unlike his buddy, Sam, who swears he gets lost in a kitchen. Wolf made some kind of stir-fry meal that was sumptuous.

I really liked his house. He said he did most of the work on it himself. It's up in the hills away from everybody. I don't guess that's very surprising. It overlooks the valley and has these great big picture windows in every room. The place has two fireplaces—one in the living room and one in the bedroom, across from this gigantic bed. Oh, and there's this huge bearskin rug in front of the fireplace. I tried to tease him about what a great entertainment spot it must be, but he didn't crack a smile. Guess he doesn't have much of a sense of humor.

We stayed Saturday night. I went on to bed and left the guys up talking. Sam told me on the way home the next afternoon that they had sat up talking until almost five o'clock! He wouldn't tell me what they were talking about—you know how close-mouthed guys are, but I could tell that Sam is worried about his friend.

I kept watching him while we were there, trying to picture the two of you together all those weeks, and quite honestly, my imagination doesn't stretch that far! I can't imagine how you stood it. You're so outgoing and friendly. Wolf rarely talks. Plus having to hike all that way. Sam found a detailed map of Colombia and had Wolf mark where he thought you guys were taken and how far you had to walk. I know that I would never have made it. Sam said he wasn't sure he could have done it, either. He's filled with admiration for you that you got through it as well as you did.

Which reminds me. How have you been feeling these days? Is the heat still bothering you? I must admit I don't miss D.C. in the summertime. Durango is a wonderful place to spend the summer months. I'm not at all sure I'm going to be able to handle the snowy winters. We'll just have to see.

Guess I'd better finish this up and get to bed. It's getting harder and harder to force myself out of bed each day to go to work. Sam and I are already talking about the possibility of starting a family before the year is out. If so, I would definitely stop working. I don't even think I would miss it.

Be sure to let us know when you can come for a visit. I can hardly wait to show you the sights. Write when you can.

Love,
Sis

Kelly read through the part about Wolf several times. He was still too thin. He seemed grimmer. Oh, Wolf! Her heart ached for him as well as for herself.

Was he having trouble falling asleep, too? Did he dream about her? Did he miss her as much as she missed him?

Kelly realized that tears were running down her cheeks. So what else was new? She had cried enough tears in the two months she'd been home to float a battleship.

She laid the letter aside and walked into the bedroom. The apartment seemed stuffy. All of Washington felt airless. There were too many people, too much pollution. There were no stars at night, no mountain vistas. Most of all, there was no Wolf.

Kelly slipped out of her clothes and walked into the bathroom. Maybe a shower would refresh her. She stood under the water for the longest time, letting the rivulets run down her body, pretending that it was Wolf touching her.

She washed her hair, thinking about cutting it. She'd gotten into the habit of wearing it in a braid on top of her head, similar to the way she had worn it in Colombia.

Forget Colombia! Forget Wolf! Get a life!

The problem was that she already had a life. Four months ago Kelly was fully convinced that she had everything she could possibly want—a wonderful job, a comfortable life-style, compatible friends, a busy social life.

Now it all seemed very boring. When she had first gone back to work it felt strange getting back into the routine. She found it a nuisance to wear hose and high heels every day, spend hours on her hair and makeup and concern herself with her appearance.

She came out of the bathroom and stretched out on the bed, remembering the waterfall where they'd first bathed, then later the lovely glade where Wolf had first made love to her. She hadn't been concerned with her appearance, she'd been too wrapped up in him.

As they usually did, her eyes fell on the large framed picture hanging on the wall opposite her bed. It was the last thing she saw at night and the first thing she saw each morning. It was a picture of Wolf.

It had been taken by the photographer just before the wedding, when Sam and Wolf were standing in the pastor's office waiting to go into the sanctuary. Wolf had been oblivious of the photographer and had obviously been kidding Sam. Sam looked very serious and very nervous. Wolf looked as though he'd just said something to Sam, teasing him, and Wolf's face was filled with light and mischief, his grin sparkling white in contrast to his tanned face.

Kelly had found the print in the enormous stack of proofs of photographs taken the day of the wedding. Everyone else had discarded it, choosing instead pictures of Sam looking like an exuberant bridegroom, with his habitual smile in place. In all those pictures, Wolf had been his habitually solemn self.

Only in this stolen moment had he shown the imp of mischief that lay hidden deep within him.

Kelly had had the picture blown up to poster size and mounted on her wall. This was how she wanted to remember Wolf. Perhaps this was not the real man. But for a little while, during brief stolen moments, this Wolf came out to play.

And he was wonderful. And she would always love him.

Kelly must have dozed off because she was awakened by the sound of her doorbell. The room was dark, and she reached over and turned on the lamp by the bed. It was almost half past eight, and she had lain down about two hours before.

Before she could sit up, the bell rang again. Still groggy, she felt for her housecoat, the one that doubled as her beach coat. Wrapping it around her, she padded out to the living room and down the hallway. Peering through the peephole, Kelly gasped in surprise.

She opened the door.

The first glimpse Wolf had of Kelly in over two months gave mute evidence that she had come to the door straight from bed. Her hair was tumbled, her legs and feet were bare, and her eyes had that drowsy look that had always made him want to kiss her senseless.

He had known he was crazy to come see her without writing or calling first. What had he expected? That she was spending her evenings pining for him?

"I'm sorry. I should have checked to see if you had company first." He started backing away from the door. "I'll give you a call tomorrow sometime and maybe—"

"Wolf! What are you talking about? You're here now. Don't go away. Come in." She held the door open for him. However, it was her uninhibited smile of welcome that completely unnerved him. She was glad to see him.

He stepped past her into her apartment. It was the first time he'd been there, although she had given him her address when they returned to the States. In addition, she had written him a short, friendly letter not long afterward, humorously relating the many adjustments she'd had to make to get used to her usual life-style.

He had never answered. He had not known what to say. He wasn't at all certain he knew what to say now. He just knew that he had had to come. He could no longer stay away.

He turned and watched her close the door. "You're looking good," he said, as much to himself as to her.

"Thank you."

"Have you gained any weight since we got back?"

She motioned him into the living room and sat down across from him. "A little. I haven't been too worried about it. How about you?"

"I don't know. I haven't paid any attention."

Now that he was sitting near a light, Kelly could see what Janet had been talking about. He did look more grim. The lines around his nose and mouth were deeper. It was all she could do to keep from leaping into his arms and smothering him with kisses.

She knew he would hate such an uninhibited demonstration. At least this Wolf would. But not the one she fantasized about. Not the one whose picture hung on her wall.

"Kelly?"

"Hmm?"

"Would you do me a favor?"

"Certainly. What?"

"Would you please go put on some clothes? That skimpy jacket really doesn't leave much to the imagination, and when you sit down, it barely covers—"

Kelly gracefully came to her feet and demurely pulled the short housecoat down around her thighs. "I didn't mean to embarrass you, Wolf. I fell asleep earlier and grabbed the first thing at hand when I heard the doorbell.''

''Then I'm glad it was me there and no one else!'' he ground out between his teeth.

She gave him a scintillating smile. ''Don't go away. I'll be right back.''

As soon as her bedroom door closed, Wolf was up and pacing. He walked over to the small kitchen area, found a glass and filled it with water, which he drank as though he'd been without liquid for days. Then he began to prowl around the room, like a caged animal looking for a way out.

He stopped and looked at every photograph she had sitting around, studied each painting on the wall, picked up table ornaments, rearranged throw pillows, looked out the windows, then began the circuit once more.

He was on his third tour of the room when the bedroom door opened and he spun around. The air suddenly left his lungs.

She wore a skimpy halter and a pair of cutoff jeans that she must have owned as a child. ''Is this better?'' she asked with a smile.

The woman didn't play fair. Not at all.

''Fine,'' he replied gruffly with an abrupt nod.

She headed toward the kitchen. ''Have you eaten?''

''Yeah.''

''Recently?''

He paused. ''I don't know.''

She stuck her head around the corner. "Let's start this conversation all over, okay? Would you like something to eat?"

"Uh, no thanks."

"Then I hope you'll excuse me because for some reason I'm starved. That's why I haven't worried about my weight. I'm always hungry these days."

He was at the entry to the kitchen area in three long strides. "You are?"

Her head was buried in the refrigerator, which placed on fine display the distracting and highly delectable shape of her derriere. "Uh-huh," came muffled from the depths of the refrigerator.

"Any particular reason?" he asked, having a little trouble with his breathing.

"Reason for what?" she asked, carrying several covered dishes and a head of lettuce to the counter.

"For being hungry all the time."

She began to open containers and place leftovers on a plate for the microwave, then made a small salad. "Oh, I don't know. Boredom, maybe. Usually the hot weather—" She stopped herself in midsentence and looked at him, looming in the doorway like some avenger. She leaned her hip against the counter and looked at him with unabashed interest. "Why do you ask?"

He shrugged. "No reason."

"Are you afraid that I might be pregnant?" she asked, twirling a curl of hair around her finger. "Because if you are, all you need to do is to ask." She went to work on her salad while he stood there watching her.

When he realized that she wasn't going to say anything else, he said, "All right, so maybe I was a little worried. I hadn't heard from you and I thought that maybe you might not— But then I thought that maybe you would— So . . . are you?"

"No."

"Oh. That's good."

She placed the plate in the oven, punched in the time necessary to heat it, then crossed her arms and turned to him. "Is it? I suppose to you it is. I'm sure you'd find it incomprehensible that someone might actually want to have a child, might hope and pray that she had gotten pregnant. That she might have cried for days and days for a baby that was never going to happen." She turned her back on him and began to pour herself some fruit juice.

"Kelly?"

She didn't answer him.

He moved closer. "Honey, I just didn't want you to be facing something alone, that's all. When I didn't hear from you—"

She spun around, green sparks flying from glittering eyes. "When you didn't *hear from me!* That's the second time you've said that. It just so happens that I wrote to you and you never bothered to answer me. So why should I continue to write you? Your silence made it clear enough that you didn't want to hear from *me.*"

"I didn't know what to say."

"Sounds like a good enough reason. You never did have much to say, as I recall."

The buzzer to the microwave went off and Kelly removed the plate, picked up her glass and marched past him into the dining area, where she sat down. She immediately got up, marched past him, got a knife and fork from a kitchen drawer, returned to the table and sat down.

She began to eat.

Wolf began pacing again.

She ignored him.

"I know this was a foolish idea, but Sam insisted I needed to come to see you."

"Why?"

"I guess to reassure myself that you were all right."

"I'm fine."

"I can see that."

She continued to eat and he continued to pace.

After she'd finished the food on her plate and drained her glass, Kelly gathered up her dishes and took them into the kitchen where she rinsed them off and placed them in the dishwasher.

"I guess you can really appreciate having all the modern conveniences after having to do without everything for so long."

"How true. I remember doing nothing but complaining day after day about the rough conditions we had, praying for the return of all my appliances, screaming that—"

"You never said a word about any of that."

"Oh. My imagination must be on the rampage again."

"You never complained about anything. You did what you were told, you trekked through miles of dripping jungle and mountains, slept on the floor in huts, camouflaged your hair and skin and never complained."

"How stoic of me."

"I've never known anyone like you, Kelly."

She shrugged. "Sure I can't get you something? Coffee? Maybe a mixed drink of some kind? I don't keep much liquor here, but if you want to keep it simple, maybe—"

"Coffee sounds good."

She began to make the coffee in silence.

"I saw Sam and Janet a couple of weeks ago."

"Yes, I know. She wrote and told me."

"What did she tell you?"

She looked over her shoulder with a puzzled expression. "Just what you said. That they went to see you."

"Anything else?"

"Uh, that you have a beautiful home, which you practically built and decorated yourself. She was particularly enamored of a certain bearskin rug in front of the bedroom fireplace."

"Yeah, she mentioned something about it."

"She also said you were a great cook, but then I already knew that."

"Did she say anything about Sam and me sitting up all night talking?"

"She mentioned it, but said Sam didn't tell her anything about the conversation."

"We talked about you."

"How boring." She poured coffee into two cups and handed him one, then led the way into the living room.

"Actually I did most of the talking."

"Until five o'clock in the morning? That doesn't sound like you."

"I know. But I needed to talk."

Kelly studied her cup thoughtfully.

"The thing is, Sam said I needed to tell you what I was telling him."

She looked up, her gaze level. "So tell me," she said gently.

"I've been trying to. I just don't know how."

"Didn't it make it easier, talking about it before... sort of like a rehearsal?"

"That's what I thought, too, right up until the time you opened the door. But the thing is, I react differently to you than I do to Sam."

"I see," she said, ducking her head and biting her lip to prevent a smile from forming.

"It's easier to talk about you than to you."

"Would it help to close your eyes?" she suggested.

He leaned his head back against the sofa as though to follow her suggestion, but he kept his eyes trained on her. "I'm really tired of fighting this thing, Kelly. I just can't keep fighting anymore."

"What are you fighting, Wolf?"

"My feelings for you."

"And what are your feelings for me?"

He cleared his throat. "I guess the worst thing is missing you. I miss you first thing in the morning as soon as I open my eyes. I miss you at night when I'm lying in bed trying to sleep. I miss watching the light dance in your eyes when you're teasing me. I even miss your teasing me. I miss the stories you make up, the outrageous stories that no one else would ever think of. I miss holding you in the night. I miss hearing your breathing, your voice, your sighs, that little purring sound you make in the back of your throat when I make love to you. I miss—"

"Okay, okay. I hear you. So you've missed me."

"Yes."

"I've missed you, too."

"You have?"

"Very much. And for pretty much the same reasons."

"Oh."

"The thing is, Wolf, what are we going to do about it?"

He shook his head. "I don't have a clue."

"Did Sam?"

"He thought I should talk to you about it."

"I see. Does that mean that you would like to hear what I have to say on the subject?"

He sighed. "I just know that I'm tired of living with this ache in my chest all the time."

Kelly placed her cup on the table next to her and stood. She walked over to Wolf, took his cup away from him, set it down and placed her hand around his.

With gentle pressure she pulled him to his feet and led him into her bedroom.

He glanced around the room with obvious interest while he followed her to the side of the bed. She turned around, letting go of his hand, and began unbuttoning his shirt.

"Kelly?"

"Hmm."

"I'm not sure that—"

"I am." She reached for his pants.

"This won't solve anything."

"But then again, it might," she pointed out reasonably. When he started to say something, she gently placed her fingers across his mouth. "Shh. I've always said that you talk too much." She pushed him gently until he sat on the side of the bed, then she knelt and pulled off his shoes.

With a couple of quick moves she had untied her halter and unfastened her shorts.

"It seems to me," she murmured, kissing him across his chest and down toward his navel, "that if we conduct our experiment in a scientific manner, we should be able to find this ache you complain of and remove it. It might take repeated applications of pressure, such as here—" she kissed him first on one nipple "—and here—" then on the other "—but in the interest of furthering scientific discovery, I would be willing to devote considerable time to the problem."

"You are a crazy woman," he muttered, grabbing her and rolling until she was pinned beneath him.

"I know." She smiled serenely up at him. "I've been crazy about you for a very long time."

Once again she knew just what to say to snap Wolf's control. He gathered her into his arms, determined that this time he would do whatever he had to in order to make certain she never left him alone again.

Wolf felt a frightening sense of déjà vu sweep over him. He'd gone through this once before, hadn't he? He had stood here at this altar, staring at a sea of interested faces, all watching him as he concentrated on not fidgeting in the rented tuxedo he wore.

Sam stood beside him, trying with great difficulty to remain solemn. Wolf prayed that his knees wouldn't betray him by buckling beneath him.

"Do you have the ring?" he whispered. Sam, the pastor and the three groomsmen echoed the word yes in unison. Okay, so he might have asked once or twice before.

Once again he watched the parade of people of all sizes coming down the aisle toward him.

What if she'd been kidnapped on the way to the church? Even though the people in charge of the last kidnapping had all been arrested, even though Kelly's father had placed a tight security surveillance around the area, Wolf could think of all kinds of things that might have happened.

And then—just as it had done once before—the organ paused in the music and began to play the wedding march. Everyone stood and faced the back of the church. Wolf wanted to shout at them to get out of his way. He couldn't see if she was there. What if—

Then he saw her, coming calmly, serenely down the aisle on her father's arm, just as though she had practiced a hundred times, rather than just once the night before.

He had never seen the dress she wore. He hadn't given the idea of her dress much thought, actually. Somewhere in the back of his mind he had thought that she might wear Janet's, but this one was Kelly, pure and simple.

The satin neckline curved down across her breasts. The waist was so tiny that she must be having trouble breathing. The skirt was cut to follow the lithe lines of her hips, thighs and legs. There was no room for a single petticoat under that skirt.

The veil covered her hair and forehead but left her eyes uncovered so that he could see them sparkling. The train fanned out behind her.

He'd never seen anyone look more beautiful. He felt as though he were going to faint.

"Hang on, you're doing fine," Sam muttered in his ear.

That's when Wolf realized that he had forgotten to breathe once he saw her.

Just as she reached him, Kelly looked into his face and smiled, her face radiant. Then she closed her left eye in a slow wink.

Kelly's eyes had fastened on Wolf as soon as she had started down the aisle a few minutes earlier. Never had he looked so grim. She knew the courage it had taken for him to reenact this scene. She knew that he had done it for her. Somehow she had to let him know that it was all right.

So she winked at him. For a moment, he looked at her in astonishment, then he grinned, the brilliant, white smile slashing across his dark face, and she saw the secret Wolf that usually stayed hidden, the Wolf of her picture, the Wolf she had fallen in love with and with whom she intended to spend the rest of her life. He was there inside the man who stood so stiffly beside her.

She had the rest of her life to coax him out to play.

Epilogue

The high country of the Guadalupe Mountains in the summer couldn't be compared to anywhere else. High above the desert floor of West Texas, the Guadalupes were part of an ancient fossil reef formed when portions of Texas and New Mexico were part of a vast tropical ocean. The forest in the high country was a relic from a time thousands of years ago when the climate was cooler and contained more moisture. As the climate warmed, parts of the forest survived in the higher elevations of the Guadalupes. Very few places offered so much contrast in a comparatively small area.

Kelly knew that she would never grow tired of spending her summers there. Nor would she ever get restless watching her family growing up with the wilderness as their second home.

She stood in the breezeway of the log cabin that she and Wolf had built several years ago and shaded her eyes, looking along the trail that led to the caves where Wolf enjoyed taking the boys.

At eight, Drew and Daniel had the energy of half a dozen half-tamed boys. Wolf had decided to give her a rest today by taking them on a long hike. They always delighted in going with him, badgering him with hundreds of questions. He seemed to take everything in stride and patiently taught them about the woods, the mountains and the world around them. They had been eager to listen to him since they had been old enough to sit and have him read to them, or to show them pictures, or take them on nature hikes.

Kelly enjoyed watching Wolf with the boys. He always seemed to have such a look of wonder and mild astonishment on his face as he watched them gambol around him like a couple of wolf pups.

She would never forget how he had acted when they brought the twins home from the hospital. He had sat by their beds for hours and stared at them as though witnessing a miracle. He told her he was afraid to take his eyes off them, in case they forgot to breathe, or perhaps choked, or cried out. She finally convinced him that between the two of them, the twins would be taken care of properly.

It had taken time, but slowly, over the years, Wolf had come to believe that he was capable of giving his children the love and guidance they needed. She was pleased to see him relaxing and enjoying them more.

She looked down at their five-year-old daughter, Marisa, and smiled. Marisa still preferred to stay close to her mother, although Wolf would have packed her on his back and taken her with them today if he could have convinced her to go with them.

Kelly watched the breeze ripple through the meadow grass and whisper through the leaves. The small valley where the cabin sat never changed. Year after year the view, the trees, even the animals that appeared at dusk to drink at the stream, looked the same.

Wolf was teaching their family about the timelessness of the wilderness that surrounded them at the same time he was teaching them the necessity of protecting what the human race had been given.

She saw movement in the distance and knew that her men were coming home. Dinner was waiting for them. As they drew closer and saw her standing there watching, the boys broke into an impromptu race, pelting across the meadow with wild whoops and yells.

Marisa looked up at Kelly with a frown. "They're actin' like a bunch of wild Injuns, Mama."

"I do believe you're right, Missy. I guess they've been watching too many Westerns."

"They don't look much like Injuns. Not like me, right, Mama?"

Kelly studied her youngest, taking in those black eyes that gazed at her with Wolf's mischievous expression and the raven black hair pulled into two braids. "That's true. Your daddy said you look just like *his* mama when you let me braid your hair like that.''

Marisa patted her hair with an important air. ''My grandma was an Indian princess, y'know.''

''Really?''

''Uh-huh. She was real pretty and everybody loved her.''

Kelly knelt and hugged her tiny daughter to her. ''If she was anything like you, darling, they couldn't have helped but love her.''

Their conversation was soon drowned out by the pounding of feet and the boys talking at the same time.

''Mom! Guess what I found? It was a fossil that looked just like a seashell. I wanted to bring it to show you but Dad said we're supposed to leave things like that where we found them so other people can see them, too.''

''Mom! Guess what? We saw this baby deer, and it was hiding behind its mama and then they started running real fast and then—''

''Mom! Did you know that there's real mountain lions up here? Really! And they hide and watch, waiting for something to walk past them, then they leap out and grab—''

''Mom! Dad said we could eat when we got home and I'm starved. Can I have something now? Just a cookie or something? Or maybe a—''

Kelly held up her hands in mock horror and began to laugh, shaking her head at the startling amount of confusion generated by the two boys.

"Hold on, wait a minute, I can't hear myself think. Maybe if you took turns I could—"

Suddenly an arm snaked around her waist from behind and she was tugged up tightly against a rock-hard body. Before she could catch her breath, a deep voice spoke low in her ear. "I do believe I've worked up quite an appetite, myself." He began to nibble along her neck, making growling sounds for the boys' benefit.

"Ah, gee, Dad, do ya have to be so mushy?"

"Mom, do baby deer make good pets?"

"Mom, is it okay if we eat now?"

"Can we go see if we can find some mountain lion tracks, Dad?"

Kelly turned in Wolf's arms and slipped her arms around his waist. "I missed you guys today. Marisa and I wandered around in all that peace and quiet, utterly lost."

He grinned, a very devilish grin with which she had become increasingly familiar over the past ten years. "I wanted you to get some rest. Besides, I thought if I took the boys out and kept them busy, they'd be so tired they would fall asleep early tonight."

"Oh? You have plans for tonight?"

"Maybe. I thought we might pick a quiet spot somewhere, lie out on a blanket and study the stars."

"Ah. One of my favorite pastimes."

He let his hand drop from her waist until it was resting against her derriere. "Mine, too," he admitted, caressing her.

She reached up and gave him a quick kiss, then turned to the three children. "All right, everybody. Get washed up. Dinner will be on the table in five minutes."

She glanced over her shoulder at Wolf. "That goes for you, too, you know."

"Yes, ma'am," he said, giving her a mock salute. Then he noticed Marisa still standing there beside her mother. "Well, if it isn't my favorite Indian princess. How would you like to go get washed up for dinner?"

Marisa cocked her head and looked at him as though she was considering his offer. "I guess," she decided. "Daddy, will you tell me a story about my grandmama who was a real Indian and lived on a reservation and—"

He picked her up and started into the house. "Honey, I think you could probably tell those stories as well as I can by now."

"Okay," she replied agreeably. "Once upon a time long ago there was this beeootiful little girl by the name of Running Deer. One day—"

Kelly was left standing alone in the breezeway, looking out across the meadow.

The children had done something for Wolf that she had not been able to do—coax him into talking more openly about his past. Once he found that the children enjoyed hearing the stories, he had found some solace in talking about his youth, making light of the pain and the loneliness, emphasizing the inner strength and self-reliance he had gained from his heritage.

It had taken time, but there had been true healing in the telling and sharing of so much that he had kept locked away inside him.

Several hours later they lay stretched out on a warm blanket in the long, soft grass of the meadow, staring at the sky.

Never had the stars seemed so bright to Kelly. She felt as though she could reach up and pluck them from the sky, but like the fossils, she decided to leave them there so that others could enjoy them.

"You warm enough?" Wolf asked, pulling her closer to him. He'd brought two blankets, one to spread over them.

"I'm fine. This was a great idea."

"Glad you approve."

"Do you ever think back to the time we were in Colombia?" she asked sleepily.

"Colombia! I haven't thought about that time in years. What made you think of it?"

"I don't know, exactly. I suppose with all the extra time on my hands today, I was reminiscing."

"Do you miss the life you had back then?"

She leaned over and looked at him. "Of course not!"

"It was certainly a far cry from being the mother of three extremely active children!"

"But you know something, Wolf. I've really enjoyed the children. Maybe I wouldn't feel the same way if we'd tried to raise them back East. But I really love our home in Albuquerque. There's plenty of space for everyone, plenty of fresh air, a place for the boys to run and kick up their heels. And you've always been there for them.''

"I intended to be. Just because you had them was no reason for you to be left to raise them.''

"I've enjoyed our life together.''

He pulled her down until her lips brushed his. "So have I. We've got a beautiful family, Kelly. One I would never have had if you hadn't come into my life.''

"Maybe we should thank Mr. Santiago for playing matchmaker.''

Wolf grabbed her and rolled until she was under him. "Are you going to talk or are you going to look at the stars?'' he growled in a teasing voice.

"I promise not to say another word.'' Instead, she kissed him.

They both missed the shooting star that sped across the low horizon. Neither one of them would have cared.

*   *   *   *   *

SILHOUETTE® *Desire*™

COMING NEXT MONTH

#667 WILD ABOUT HARRY—Linda Lael Miller
Widowed mom Amy Ryan was sure she wasn't ready to love again.
But why was she simply wild about Australia's *Man of the World*,
Harry Griffith?

#668 A FINE MADNESS—Kathleen Korbel
It seemed someone thought that England's *Man of the World*,
Matthew Spears, and Quinn Rutledge belonged together! Could they
survive an eccentric ghost's matchmaking antics and discover
romance on their own?

#669 ON HIS HONOR—Lucy Gordon
When Italy's *Man of the World*, Carlo Valetti, walked back into
Serena Fletcher's life, she was nervous. Was this sexy charmer there
to claim *her* love—or *his* daughter?

#670 LION OF THE DESERT—Barbara Faith
Morocco's *Man of the World*, Sheik Kadim al-Raji, had a mission—
to rescue Diane St. James from kidnappers. But once they were safe,
would this primitive male be able to let her go?

#671 FALCONER—Jennifer Greene
Shy Leigh Merrick knew life was no fairy tale, but then she met
Austria's *Man of the World*, roguish Rand Krieger. This lord of the
castle sent her heart soaring....

#672 SLADE'S WOMAN—BJ James
Fragile Beth Warren never dreamed she'd ever meet anyone like
America's *Man of the World*, Hunter Slade. But this solitary man just
wanted to be left alone....

AVAILABLE NOW:

#661 PRIDE AND JOY
Joyce Thies

#662 OUT OF DANGER
Beverly Barton

#663 THE MIDAS TOUCH
Cathryn Clare

#664 MUSTANG VALLEY
Jackie Merritt

#665 SMOOTH SAILING
Cathie Linz

#666 LONE WOLF
Annette Broadrick

Bestselling author NORA ROBERTS captures all the
romance, adventure, passion and excitement of Silhouette in
a special miniseries.

THE
CALHOUN WOMEN

Four charming, beautiful and fiercely independent
sisters set out on a search for a missing family
heirloom—an emerald necklace—and each finds
something even more precious . . . passionate romance.

Look for THE CALHOUN WOMEN miniseries
starting in June.

COURTING CATHERINE
in Silhouette Romance #801 (June/$2.50)

A MAN FOR AMANDA
in Silhouette Desire #649 (July/$2.75)

FOR THE LOVE OF LILAH
in Silhouette Special Edition #685 (August/$3.25)

SUZANNA'S SURRENDER
in Silhouette Intimate Moments #397 (September/$3.29)

 *Silhouette Books*®

Silhouette Special Edition

presents

SONNY'S GIRLS

by Emilie Richards, Celeste Hamilton and Erica Spindler

They had been Sonny's girls, irresistibly drawn to the charismatic high school football hero. Ten years later, none could forget the night that changed their lives forever.

In July—
ALL THOSE YEARS AGO by Emilie Richards (SSE #684)
Meredith Robbins had left town in shame. Could she ever banish the past and reach for love again?

In August—
DON'T LOOK BACK by Celeste Hamilton (SSE #690)
Cyndi Saint was Sonny's steady. Ten years later, she remembered only his hurtful parting words....

In September—
LONGER THAN... by Erica Spindler (SSE #696)
Bubbly Jennifer Joyce was everybody's friend. But nobody knew the secret longings she felt for bad boy Ryder Hayes....

"INDULGE A LITTLE" SWEEPSTAKES

HERE'S HOW THE SWEEPSTAKES WORKS

NO PURCHASE NECESSARY

To enter each drawing, complete the appropriate Official Entry Form or a 3" by 5" index card by hand-printing your name, address and phone number and the trip destination that the entry is being submitted for (i.e., Walt Disney World Vacation Drawing, etc.) and mailing it to: Indulge '91 Subscribers-Only Sweepstakes, P.O. Box 1397, Buffalo, New York 14269-1397.

No responsibility is assumed for lost, late or misdirected mail. Entries must be sent separately with first class postage affixed, and be received by: 9/30/91 for the Walt Disney World Vacation Drawing, 10/31/91 for the Alaskan Cruise Drawing and 11/30/91 for the Hawaiian Vacation Drawing. Sweepstakes is open to residents of the U.S. and Canada, 21 years of age or older as of 11/7/91.

For complete rules, send a self-addressed, stamped (WA residents need not affix return postage) envelope to: Indulge '91 Subscribers-Only Sweepstakes Rules, P.O. Box 4005, Blair, NE 68009.

© 1991 HARLEQUIN ENTERPRISES LTD.   DIR-RL

"INDULGE A LITTLE" SWEEPSTAKES

HERE'S HOW THE SWEEPSTAKES WORKS

NO PURCHASE NECESSARY

To enter each drawing, complete the appropriate Official Entry Form or a 3" by 5" index card by hand-printing your name, address and phone number and the trip destination that the entry is being submitted for (i.e., Walt Disney World Vacation Drawing, etc.) and mailing it to: Indulge '91 Subscribers-Only Sweepstakes, P.O. Box 1397, Buffalo, New York 14269-1397.

No responsibility is assumed for lost, late or misdirected mail. Entries must be sent separately with first class postage affixed, and be received by: 9/30/91 for the Walt Disney World Vacation Drawing, 10/31/91 for the Alaskan Cruise Drawing and 11/30/91 for the Hawaiian Vacation Drawing. Sweepstakes is open to residents of the U.S. and Canada, 21 years of age or older as of 11/7/91.

For complete rules, send a self-addressed, stamped (WA residents need not affix return postage) envelope to: Indulge '91 Subscribers-Only Sweepstakes Rules, P.O. Box 4005, Blair, NE 68009.

© 1991 HARLEQUIN ENTERPRISES LTD.   DIR-RL

INDULGE A LITTLE—WIN A LOT!

Summer of '91 Subscribers-Only Sweepstakes

OFFICIAL ENTRY FORM

This entry must be received by: Sept. 30, 1991
This month's winner will be notified by: Oct. 7, 1991
Trip must be taken between: Nov. 7, 1991—Nov. 7, 1992

YES, I want to win the Walt Disney World® vacation for two. I understand the prize includes round-trip airfare, first-class hotel and pocket money as revealed on the "wallet" scratch-off card.

Name _____

Address_____ Apt. _____

City _____

State/Prov. _____ Zip/Postal Code _____

Daytime phone number _____
(Area Code)

Return entries with invoice in envelope provided. Each book in this shipment has two entry coupons—and the more coupons you enter, the better your chances of winning!

© 1991 HARLEQUIN ENTERPRISES LTD.   CPS-M1